A CANDLELIGHT ROMANCE

CANDLELIGHT ROMANCES

Morning Rose, Evening Savage

Amii Lorin

A CANDLELIGHT ROMANCE

Published by
Dell Publishing Co., Inc.
1 Dag Hammarskjold Plaza
New York, New York 10017

Dell ® TM 681510, Dell Publishing Co., Inc.

ISBN: 0-440-15568-1

Printed in the United States of America

First printing—August 1980

CHAPTER ONE

Tara's fingers flew over the keys of the humming Olivetti, her eyes steady on the letter she was transcribing. So intent was her concentration, she didn't hear the office door open and she glanced up with a start when the morning mail was dropped onto the corner of her desk.

"Coffee's just about ready, Tara," Jeannie, the young file clerk and head coffee-maker, caroled brightly. "I'll be back with it in a minute, okay?"

Fingers hovering over the keys, Tara nodded and returned the smile of the pretty, eager teen-ager.

"Yes, thank you. I'm just finishing the last of the letters David left. I can take a few minutes and relax with my coffee while I go through the mail."

Jeannie nodded and bounced out of the office and Tara went back to the keyboard. She finished the letter, placed it on top of the others she'd typed that morning, then flexed her fingers and arched her back in a stretching motion.

Glancing at the clock, she noted it was nine forty and she'd been typing steadily since eight. On entering her office at her usual time, a few minutes before eight, she'd found her typewriter uncovered and a piece of paper rolled into it on which her boss had typed:

Tara,

I have an early appointment. Type up these letters I dashed off last night, if you can decipher them. I should be in the office around ten.

David

Tara smiled to herself. *Decipher* had been the correct word. Though David's architectural drawings were a beautiful sight to behold, one might suspect from his handwriting he was a doctor.

Tara had come to work for the young architect on leaving secretarial college four years ago and the atmosphere had always been informal. From the first day it had been *Tara* and *David*, never *Miss Schmitt* and *Mr. Jennings*. There had been a smaller staff at the time as David had just begun receiving recognition for his work, but as David's reputation grew, so had his staff. Yet the informality remained.

Jeannie delivered the coffee and, after taking a careful sip, Tara gave a small, contented sigh. From the very first day she had considered herself fortunate in finding this job. She enjoyed the work, earned an excellent salary, and, perhaps the best of all, she had made firm friendships with David and his wife, Sallie.

Sallie had acted as David's secretary until she was in her seventh month of pregnancy with their first child. She had remained in the office one week after Tara started, to show her the office procedure. In that short time they discovered a rapport that grew into a strong bond between them.

As for David, Tara freely admitted to herself that, if he had not been married, she would have made a play for him. David Jennings was one of the few men Tara really liked. His looks were commonplace. Tall and thin, almost to the point of gauntness, he had thinning, sandy-colored hair and wore dark-framed glasses. His manner was gentle, with a smile that could melt the core of an iceberg. At the same time he was a brilliant architect and an unabashed workaholic.

Tara rose and walked around the desk to ease her cramped legs, then stood with her back to the door as she flipped through the mail. The office door opened then closed quietly and Tara went stiff at the sound of the new familiar, deeply masculine voice of David's newest, and so far most important, client. "I understand you're looking around for a prosperous man to marry. Would I fill the requirements?"

Shock, followed by swift anger at the softly insolent tone, stiffened her spine even more. Jerking her head up, she turned swiftly to glare into the handsome, mocking face of Aleksei Rykovsky.

"If you are trying to be funny," Tara snapped, "you are failing miserably."

Eyes as deeply blue and glittering as sapphires roamed her face slowly, studying with amusement the high angry color in her creamy cheeks, the flash of sparks in her dark brown eyes, the way she flipped back her long silvery gold hair in agitation.

"Not at all," he finally answered in a silky smooth tone. "I am completely serious. Have I been misinformed about your avowed intention to marry a man who is—uh—well-off?"

Tara was not a small girl, standing five feet nine in her three-inch heels, yet she had to tilt back her head to look into his face. *And what a face,* she thought sourly. For any one man to possess such a devastatingly rugged handsomeness was unfair to the rest of the male population in general and to the whole of the female population in particular. The face was the icing on the cake, being at the top of a long, muscularly lean body that exuded pure male vitality and sensuousness. And as if that were not enough, a full head of crisp, blue-black wavy hair was a blatant invitation to feminine fingers. *Too bad,* Tara thought in the same sour vein, *his personality is a complete turnoff.* She did not appreciate the masterful type.

"No," she finally managed to answer, forcing herself to meet that steady blue gaze. "You have not been misinformed."

"Well, then," he drawled, "all we have to do is set the date."

Tara felt the flash of angry color touch her skin. If there was anything she hated more than an arrogant man, it was to be made the object of his humor. She breathed in deeply, trying to keep a rein on her growing temper. For David's sake, she could not afford to antagonize this man.

"You've had your little joke for the day, Mr. Rykovsky," she said through stiff lips, "now if you'll excuse me, I have work to do and—"

"Morning, Tara." David's cheerful voice preceded him into the room. The rest of him followed, a warm smile lightening his otherwise nondescript face. "Have any trouble with my chicken scratches?"

8

"Not too much." Tara smiled at her boss, sighing in relief at his appearance. "They're all typed and ready for your signature."

David grinned at the other man as she handed him the neatly typed sheets. "Every busy man should have a Tara in his office, Alek." Then, turning, he walked to the door of his own office. Before following, Alek leaned close to Tara and whispered, "I can think of a better place to have you." Then he moved quickly up behind David, who turned and said, "Alek and I are going to be closeted the rest of the day, Tara. I don't want to be disturbed unless it's something you think absolutely must have my attention."

Struck speechless by Alek's whispered words, she nodded dumbly, then stood still, watching the door close. Tara's thoughts exploded. *How dared he, that—that arrogant, overbearing, conceited*—words failed her. Unclenching her hands, flexing stiff, achy fingers, she made a concentrated effort at control. The emotions raging through her were an equal mixture of anger and humiliation. Anger at his audacity at using her to sharpen his—to her mind—twisted wit. Humiliation at the fact that the basis of his attack was true: she *had* promised herself she'd marry a prosperous man. And although it was ten years since she'd made the vow, she had not changed her mind in the least.

Legs still shaky, Tara walked slowly around her desk and sank into her chair. In a burst of activity she got busy with the work at hand only to pause moments later to stare unseeingly at her typewriter.

She had been fourteen when she'd made that vow, a not unusual thing at that romantic age. Most young girls have been known to declare dreamily that they

9

will marry rich men. But, unlike other girls, Tara had had no dreams of a prince charming with gold-lined pockets. Quite the contrary. She had viewed the prospect realistically. A handsome Prince Charming she didn't need; actual wealth she didn't need. What she had decided she wanted was a reasonably prosperous man and, of equal importance, one who would not be a tyrant. She had already, at the tender age of fourteen, seen enough of the type of man who, to feed his own ego, had to be forever boss. She had seen him in her male teachers, in the fathers of most of her friends, and in her own father.

Tara shuddered as a picture of her mother thrust its unwelcome way into her mind. Trying to dispel the unwanted image, she got to work. She was only partially successful, for throughout the rest of the day incidents and scenes from her childhood flashed in and out of her mind. And her mother was in every one: her beauty fading over the years; her bright eyes growing dim and shadowed with worry; her flashing smile turning into a mere twist of once full lips that had felt the bite of teeth too often; and, possibly the worst of all, shoulders starting to bow with the weight of hardship and far too little appreciation.

Not for me, Tara had told herself while still in her ninth year of school. *Not for me the scrimping and scraping to make ends meet but rarely even coming close. Not for me the tyrant who would be absolute master in his home, punishing his wife for his own inadequacies.*

She had indulged in no wild dreams or flights of fancy, but had planned carefully and well. She had been blessed with beauty of both face and body and she nurtured it rigidly, getting plenty of rest and exercise and being very careful of what she ate. She had worked at baby-sitting and as a mother's helper from the time she was thirteen, giving most of her earnings to her mother, but always managing to put aside a few dollars for herself. At sixteen she got a regular job working part-time after school in the winter and full-time in the summer. She paid a rather high board at home and hoarded the rest of her money like a miser. She studied hard, receiving high grades in school. After graduation she had applied at and was accepted into a highly reputable secretarial college in Philadelphia, whose curriculum included courses on charm and personal appearance. She bolstered her funds by working part-time at Gimbels department store. It had not been easy. In fact it had been very difficult. But it had paid off. When she left secretarial school at twenty, she came home to Allentown a beautiful, poised, well-groomed, excellently trained secretary.

She was hired for the first job she applied for, the one in David's office. That had been four years ago. The first two of those years she lived at home, wanting to ease the burden on her mother. But the situation became increasingly more impossible. She found it harder to except her father's dictates. She was no longer a green girl, but a well turned-out, highly paid young woman and she could no longer bear being told when to come and when to go, when to speak and when to be silent. A few days after her twenty-second birthday she packed her things and left her father's house for good.

She did not actively hate her father. Herman Schmitt did the best he could within the range of his own knowledge and understanding. What his firstborn daughter resented was that he'd never made an effort to widen his vision past what he'd learned of life from his own straight-laced, Pennsylvania Dutch parents. And more important still, she resented his marrying a lovely, laughing, blond-haired girl and turning her into a nervous, drawn-faced, gray-haired, timid mouse.

No. No. No. Not for Tara this type of man and life. Over the years her resolve had strengthened. It had not taken long for her co-workers and few close friends to ascertain her goals. She rarely dated and then only with carefully selected young men. She was wise enough to realize one had little control over the unpredictable emotion called love. So she operated within the premise that she could not become vulnerable to the wrong man if she had no contact with him. None of the men she'd dated over the years had left an impression on her, and at the present time she wasn't seeing anyone.

She had no idea who had enlightened Aleksei Rykovsky as to her intentions. Who it was did not even matter. What did matter was that that hateful man had used it to amuse himself at her expense.

Tara had felt an immediate antagonism toward him from the day, a few months ago, that David had introduced her to him. He wore his breeding, wealth, and self-confidence like a banner. Arrogance etched every fine, aristocratic feature of his dark-skinned, handsome face. This man, she had thought at once, was probably the most bossy of any boss she had ever met. She hadn't liked him then; she liked him even less now.

The afternoon wore on, her thoughts and memories occasionally jarred by the sound of a low, masculine voice that sometimes filtered through the closed door.

Tara greeted quitting time with a sigh of weariness, and slid one slim hand under the heavy fall of silver-blond hair to rub the back of her neck. She tidied her desk, covered her typewriter, slipped into her light-weight suede jacket, scooped up her shoulder bag, and left the office with unusual haste. As she walked to the parking lot, she drew deep lungsful of crisp October air in an attempt to clear her mind of the afternoon cobwebs. She unlocked the door of her six-month-old blue Camaro and, her sense of well-being returning, she slid behind the wheel, started the engine, and drove off the parking lot and into the crowded line of homebound traffic. In her preoccupied state she didn't hear the low roar of the engine being started up after hers, or notice the shimmery, beetle-green Thunderbird that followed her off the lot.

Fifteen minutes later she had left the heavier traffic and five minutes after that she parked the car on the quiet street in front of her apartment house. Thanking the Fates it was Friday, she locked the car, slung the handbag strap over her shoulder, and hurried across the sidewalk and through the street door of the apartment, unaware of the same Thunderbird parked two cars away from her own.

Dashing up the stairs, she swung into the hall, heading for her second floor apartment, then stopped dead in her tracks. Leaning against the wall next to her front door was the cause of her suddenly intense headache. Looking for all the world like he owned the place stood one totally relaxed Aleksei Rykovsky.

Tara felt anger reignite and the flame propelled

13

her forward. She stopped a foot from him, brown eyes smoldering. "What are you doing here?"

Dark eyebrows went up in exaggerated surprise. "I thought we had things to discuss." His voice flowed over her like smooth honey, and she felt a tiny shiver slide along her spine.

"We have nothing to discuss," she snapped irritably. "Now, if you'll excuse me, I'm tired." She had turned and unlocked the door while she was speaking, preparing to step inside and close the door in his face, when his voice stopped her. "Of course if you're afraid to talk to me . . ."

Tara turned, her eyes frosty, her face mirroring contempt. "I'm not afraid to talk to any man. What is it you have to say?"

"I usually don't hold conversations in hallways. May I come in?" The taunting amusement in his voice grated on her nerves and, with an exclamation of annoyance, she flung open the door, then spun around and walked into the living room.

On hearing the door close with a soft click, she drew a deep breath for control then turned to watch him come slowly across the room to her.

"What do you want?"

"You."

Tara's breath was drawn in on an audible gasp. "Are you out of your mind?"

"No more than most. If I'm not mistaken, I proposed marriage to you today. I came for an answer."

"No."

"Why?"

Really angry now, Tara was finding it difficult keeping her voice down. "I told you this morning I don't think you're funny. Aren't you carrying this joke a bit too far?"

"And I told you this morning I was not trying to be funny." His own tone wasn't quite as smooth. "I mean it. Will you marry me?"

Tara brushed her hand across her eyes in disbelief. "Why? I mean, why are you asking me to marry you?"

He stepped closer to her, brought up one hand to brush long brown fingers across her soft cheek. "Fair question," he murmured, "but I've already answered it. You're a beautiful, desirable woman. I want you. Would you let me set you up in an apartment in my building?"

"No." It was a soft explosive uttered at the same time she moved back, away from his caressing, oddly disturbing fingers.

"I thought not." He laughed low in his throat, arching one mocking brow at her as she moved away from him. "If the only way I can have you is through marriage," he shrugged, "I'll marry you. I should more than meet your requirements of a prosperous man. I'm a very, very prosperous man."

Tara shivered in revulsion. This man's arrogance was beyond belief.

"Get out of here." Her voice had dropped to a whisper, and she was shaking in anger.

"Tara."

"If you don't get out of here, I'll call the super and have you thrown out." Fighting for control, she spoke through clenched teeth.

Dark blue eyes, bright and glittering with anger, stared into hers; then he moved so quickly, she was left speechless. His hands shot out and caught her face, drawing her up to him. Up. Up, until she was

15

almost dangling on tiptoes inches below his face. She could do no more with her hands than grasp his waist for support, and her voice was a barely strangled gasp.

"What do you think you're—"

Closing the inches that separated them, he caught her open mouth with his, sending a shaft of sensation Tara later told herself was disgust through her body that left the tips of her fingers and toes tingling. His lips were firm, cool, and insistent and, to her horror, she felt her own begin to respond.

Alek's mouth released her slowly. Then with his lips still almost touching hers, she felt his cool breath mingle with hers as he murmured words in a strange language Tara thought must be Russian. His mouth brushed hers roughly before he lifted his head, and his even more darkened blue eyes stared into her soft brown ones, wide with confusion and a hint of fear. "All right, pansy eyes, I'll go," he said softly, then more firmly, "but think about what I said. I could give you a very comfortable life, Tara."

He released her so suddenly, she almost fell, and before she could form a retort, he was across the room and out the door. Trembling with reaction, lips parted to draw deep, steadying breaths, she glanced around the room as if seeking reassurance from familiar things. *No one in his right mind would say and do the things he had,* she thought wildly. Moving a little unsteadily, she walked to the sofa and sank into it, resting her head back and closing her eyes. *The man had to be mad.* The thought jolted her memory back to something David had said months ago.

Tara had had dinner with David and Sallie and they'd been sitting comfortably in the living room with their coffee when Sallie mentioned Aleksei

Rykovsky. Tara had grimaced with distaste and, with a rueful smile, David shook his head. "I don't understand why you don't like him, Tara. Most people do, you know."

Although David and Sallie had long been aware of Tara's preference for well-off men and in fact had introduced her to a few (believing she had an ingrained fear of being poor due to her upbringing), they had no idea of her aversion to the masterful type.

Tara had sighed, reluctant to answer, yet knowing she had to say something. "Oh, I don't know. It's just, well, he seems so damned sure of himself. So completely *in charge. The*"—and here she waved her hand around as if trying to pluck the word out of the air— "*boss,* so to speak. It annoys me."

"I don't know why it should," came David's gentle-voiced reply. "I've never heard him boss you. And anyway, he is the boss. You know what designing his new plant means to me, Tara. This is what I've been waiting for ever since I opened my own office. This is the biggest challenge I've had so far, and Alek has very definite ideas on what he does and does not want. My God, girl, you've seen the proposed budget. In my view, any man who can afford to build a new plant at that cost without batting an eye damned well deserves to be boss."

David's tone had become unusually severe toward the end of his admonition to Tara, and when he finished, the room grew taut with a strained silence.

In an obvious attempt to lighten the mood, Sallie turned to David with a soft laugh. "Darling, within the last few weeks I've heard several people refer to

17

him as 'the Mad Russian.' Do you have any idea why?"

David's laughter echoed his wife's, and when he answered, all traces of his previous harshness were gone. "Yes, sweets, I do know why. But don't be alarmed; they don't mean crazy-mad. It seems Alek has acquired a reputation for accepting difficult jobs with a close delivery date. Real squeakers, so to speak. The way I hear it, he has, so far, always managed to deliver top quality work—on time. When he first started this practice, those who are in a position to know were heard to say the man was mad to take on such impossible job orders. Ergo—the title *Mad Russian* evolved."

Sallie gave an exaggerated sigh of relief. "Well, that's good to know. I was beginning to think perhaps his attic light was out."

Opening her eyes, Tara shuddered and sat up, Sallie's words of months ago ringing in her ears. After Aleksei Rykovsky's behavior this evening, Tara was inclined to disregard David's explanation and go with Sallie's. In Tara's opinion the Mad Russian's attic light was definitely out.

Reaction was setting in. Tara felt tight and jumpy all over and, glancing down, she stared vacantly at her trembling hands. Closing her eyes, she swallowed around the dryness in her throat and bit hard on her lower lip.

Suddenly she had to move, needed the feeling of some sort of purposeful action. Moving almost jerkily, she went into the kitchen to the cabinet where she kept her cleaning materials. Grasping a dustcloth and a can of spray wax, she returned to the living room.

Slowly, methodically, she applied herself to waxing

18

every piece of wooden furniture in the room. There were not all that many pieces, for it wasn't a very large room. But what there was was well chosen, reflecting Tara's quiet good taste. Not an edge or corner was missed and from there Tara went into the bedroom and proceeded to give the same treatment to the furniture there.

When, finally, she had to admit to herself there was not one square inch of wood left without a double coat of wax, she returned to the kitchen and replaced the cloth and can.

Straightening from the low cabinet, she stood motionless a moment then said aloud, wonderingly, "What am I doing?" But without allowing any answers to filter through, she was moving again, going to the sink to wash her hands.

Uneasy, because she didn't know why, Tara didn't want to think at all just then. Least of all about *him*.

With single-minded purpose she broiled a small steak, tossed an equally small salad, and brewed half a pot of coffee. Twenty-five minutes after she had seated herself at the small kitchen table, she swallowed the last of her third cup of coffee then stood up and carried her plate to the sink to scrape most of her meal into the garbage disposal.

Tara washed up slowly and carefully, wiping the table, countertops, and stove free of the tiniest imagined spot. When she finally flicked the light switch off, she left the darkened room even more neat and sparkling than usual.

Still moving with the same single-minded purpose, she went to the bathroom, stripped, stepped under the shower, and brought all her concentration to bear

19

on shampooing her long, heavy fall of silver-blond hair.

Later, dressed in nightie and terry robe, she sat in front of her makeup mirror—brush in one hand, blow dryer in the other—and stared with unseeing eyes into the glass. In her mind's eye grew a sharp picture of two glittering dark blue eyes and inside her head, as clearly as a few hours earlier, that deep masculine voice said: "You're a beautiful, desirable woman. I want you."

A shudder went through her body, and she watched, almost blankly, her pale, slim hand grasp the handle of the dryer to still its shaking.

He was beyond her experience. His manner—everything about him—was an unknown. She had gone out with a few carefully selected young men. She had been kissed, thoroughly, by all of them. Most had made a play toward a more intimate relationship. Yet none had shocked or upset her as this man had, with seemingly little effort.

Tara felt vaguely frightened even now, hours later, and she wasn't quite sure why. Was she overreacting? She didn't think so. People who were hitting on all cylinders didn't behave as he had. Did they?

From their first meeting she had felt uncomfortable and strangely on edge whenever he was around, either in the office or on the building site, and now, Tara told herself, she knew why. Not only was he autocratic and arrogant, which were bad enough in themselves, but he also had a streak of erraticism. The thing that puzzled her was, if she had sensed this in the man, why hadn't David and the others?

CHAPTER TWO

Tara had a depressing weekend. Not only was she shaken, at odd hours of the day and night, by thoughts of Aleksei Rykovsky's strange behavior, she made the mistake of choosing this weekend to visit her mother.

She walked into her father's house Sunday after dinner to find her mother in tears, her father bellowing at her younger sister, Betsy, and the twenty-one-year-old Betsy screaming back that she was packing her clothes and moving in with her boyfriend.

Tara groaned softly as she hurried across the room to her mother. *This was all I needed to make my weekend complete,* she thought wearily. At that moment she would not have been shocked or surprised if her mother told her her eighteen-year-old brother George had a girl in trouble and that her fourteen-year-old-brother Karl had taken their father's car and smashed it.

"Tara." Her mother grasped her arms agitatedly. "Please go talk to your sister. She'll listen to you. I'll die of shame if she moves in with Kenny. And your father will be impossible to live with."

So what else is new, Tara thought resignedly. But she smoothed her mother's once beautiful hair, then gently removed her clutching hands. "All right, Mama, I'll go see what I can do. But will you tell me what this is all about first?" As she was speaking she drew her mother into the kitchen, enabling them to talk without having to shout over the din from the second floor.

In the comparative quiet of the kitchen, Marlene Schmitt drew a deep breath before beginning her explanations. "Well, it started Friday," she began and Tara thought swiftly, didn't everything? "Your father told Betsy that with inflation and all, he'd have to raise her board. She was very upset because she herself hasn't had a raise in pay for some time. Then yesterday they had an argument just before Kenny came for her to go to a movie. He said her room looked like a pigsty, and it was time she cleaned it." Tara felt a flash of irritation. It was true that Betsy was a little careless with her things, but her room did not look like a pigsty.

"They barely spoke to each other all morning." Her mother's eyes filled with tears, and she twisted her hands nervously. "I guess it's my fault. I was late with dinner, and Betsy asked if she could skip drying the dishes since Kenny was picking her up soon and she had to get ready. Your father exploded. He told her she was not allowed to go with Kenny today and could only see him two nights a week from now on."

"For heaven's sake, Mother, Betsy's twenty-one years old," Tara exclaimed indignantly.

"That's exactly what she said to him. But he told her that she was in his house, and as long as she remained under his roof, she'd do as he said. That's when she said she wouldn't stay here any longer.

22

That she was moving in with Kenny. Oh, Tara, please stop her."

"Okay, okay, calm down. I said I'd do what I can. And you're not to blame yourself just because dinner was late. I'll talk to him too, if I can, and try to make him see reason."

Several hours later Tara collapsed onto her own sofa with a sigh of exhaustion. After long talks with both her sister and father that would have put a diplomat to shame, she had finally procured a peace settlement of sorts. She smiled ruefully, acknowledging the fact that George had been the one who swayed her father. He had entered the house, and the argument, and declared firmly in favor of Betsy. That her eighteen-year-old brother's opinion was held in higher esteem by her father than her own did not surprise Tara. To a man like her father the judgment of almost any male held more value than that of a female. With bitter amusement Tara thought her father would fall over one Aleksei Rykovsky, seeing in him the absolute top dog of dominant men. Her amusement faded as she considered the probability of encountering that same top dog in the office tomorrow. After Friday night, what could they possibly say to each other? How could they work together if need be?

Thankfully her fears were proved groundless—at least through Wednesday—as the "head honcho," as Tara now thought of him, hadn't appeared.

A mystery did, though, in the form of a single, long-stemmed white rose that was delivered to her at the office Monday morning and each morning after that. When Jeannie brought the first one to her, Tara was at first delighted. The rose was perfectly shaped and beautiful; its scent heady, almost sensual. As

23

Tara searched through the tissue paper in the florist box, Jeannie sighed enviously. "You must have a secret admirer, Tara. The delivery man said there was no card and wouldn't even take a tip. Said he'd already been tipped. Do you have any idea who it's from?"

Tara shook her head slowly. "No, but I'll probably find out before too long." Then smiling teasingly at the younger girl, she added, "And you'll be the first to know, I promise."

Jeannie flashed her an impish grin as she left the office, and Tara sat staring broodingly at the rose. Who could have sent it? The first name to jump into her mind was Aleksei Rykovsky, but she dismissed that at once. Much too subtle for the head honcho; he apparently went in for caveman tactics. Who then? Terry Connors? She mused on the young draftsman in the outer office a few moments, then shook her head decisively. Not Terry. He probably wouldn't think of it, especially after the way she'd spoken to him the last time he'd asked her out. She'd been honest to the point of bluntness. Although he was an attractive young man with talent and a promising future, he was more in love with himself than he could be with any one woman. In so many words she'd told him just that. He'd barely spoken to her since and then only in the office. He lived in an apartment just down the street from hers, and she'd passed him a few times going to and from her apartment and her car. At those times he'd nodded curtly, not speaking. So scratch Terry.

Names kept bouncing in and out of her mind as she hunted up the summer bud vase she'd shoved to the back of her personal desk drawer, and one by one she rejected them. Finally, running out of prospects, she gave up.

She went through the same mental gyrations on Tuesday morning. When the rose was delivered on Wednesday morning, she decided to stop trying to solve the puzzle and just enjoy it.

As she prepared for bed Wednesday night Tara realized the advent of the morning rose had taken the edge off her nervousness about meeting Aleksei Rykovsky in the office. She also told herself the man was probably feeling ridiculous about his behavior and had not come to David's office because he was embarrassed to face her. She should have known better.

She was at the filing cabinet Thursday morning when David, with a pleasant good morning, breezed through her small office on the way to his own. Tara looked up, but before she had a chance to voice a return greeting, two strong hands gripped her shoulders and a caressing voice said, "Morning, darling," as she was turned around and held against a hard, muscular chest. She saw gleaming blue eyes, gave a startled "Oh," then went warm all over as Aleksei Rykovsky's firm mouth covered hers. Again that odd, tingling sensation touched the tips of her fingers and toes but before she could react to push him away, he lifted his head. "I missed that this morning, sleepyhead." While caressing, his tone also held a touch of possession, and Tara was left speechless. He laughed softly as he moved away from her with obvious reluctance to join David, who still stood in the doorway with a patently interested look on his face.

Flushed with embarrassment, wide-eyed in confusion, Tara faced David. "I—I . . ."

David shook his head slowly, smiled gently, and closed the door between the two offices.

Anger flushed her cheeks even more brightly as she stared at the closed door. Who did he think he was, kissing her like that? And what in the world did he mean, he'd missed that this morning?

At lunchtime, instead of having lunch at her desk as she usually did, Tara left the office and walked. Ever since her teens, whenever she was troubled or had a particularly knotty problem to work out, she walked. She started out at a good pace, her long slender legs eating up the city blocks rapidly. Anger stirred her blood and kept the adrenaline pumping.

This man, this Rykovsky, was beginning to drive her wild. *Banish him,* she told herself severely. *Push him out of your mind completely.* Not an easy thing to do. Mocking blue eyes in a handsome face were beginning to haunt her. Why had he suddenly set out to bedevil her? Had she slipped up, let her dislike and disapproval of him show? If she had, she couldn't think when. For David's sake she had worked hard at always displaying a cool, efficient, respectful attitude toward him.

She could not think of one instance during the last few months when she had let her mask drop even at the times—and there had been several during office meetings and on the new plant site—when his overbearing superiority, his enormous self-confidence and arrogance, had made her hand itch with the desire to slap his haughty, patrician face. She had controlled the urge by removing herself from his presence on one pretext or another.

Sighing softly, Tara shook her head in defeat. She had no idea why he was attacking her. She had avoided his type like the plague and so could not fathom what his motivation could possibly be.

Tara had been striding along at a good clip, oblivious to her surroundings and the gloriously warm fall day. The dry, crackling sound of leaves being crushed underfoot cracked the door of her consciousness; the happy ripple of young children laughing pushed it open.

Glancing around, she shortened her stride; then she stopped completely. She was passing the park, the still deep-green, well tended grass partially obscured now by the heavy fall of leaves from the various types of trees in the park. Again children laughing caught her attention, and her gaze followed the sounds to the park's small-tot lot. Young mothers stood together talking while keeping a watchful eye on their offspring. Others guided toddlers down sliding boards or stood behind swings, gently pushing each time the seat arced back. Bemused, Tara watched the happy, worry-free youngsters play. She had always loved children, been happy and eager to help her mother when first George and then Karl were born.

A gentle smile tugged at her lips; a tiny ache tugged at her heart. Would she ever meet a man whose children she would not only be willing to raise but wanted to bear with a deep and passionate longing? Had she set her sights too high, made her requirements too rigid? Apparently not, for she had met more than one young man who'd not only met her requirements but had other extra added attractions as well. Yet they had all left her cold, with no desire to continue the relationship, let alone deepen it.

Was she destined to spend the rest of her life alone,

searching for some illusive thing that could set a spark to her emotions? Was she never to know the joy evident on the faces of the young mothers she now observed? Did they realize, she wondered, how precious the time was that they held in their hands as their babies grew? Did anyone ever?

Giving herself a mental shake, Tara breathed in deeply, filling her lungs with the sweet, smoky taste of autumn. She had become pensive and moody and, with a determined effort, she drew her eyes away from the children, turned, and began retracing her steps to the office.

A long, low wolf-whistle, issued from the window of a passing car, brought a smile to Tara's lips, a spring to her step. Her long, silvery hair bounced on her shoulders and against her back in rhythm with her stride. The soft breeze played havoc with the feather-cut hair that curved down, then flipped back on either side of her center part.

Her walk—*or stalk,* Tara thought wryly—had restored her equilibrium. For all of fifteen minutes, back there at the park, she hadn't given one thought to the head honcho. But now he was back to torment her thoughts. She had walked off the sharpest edge of her anger, but the core was still there, burning low but steadily.

What games was this man playing at? And how in the world would she explain her behavior this morning to David? Her worry on that score proved groundless, for she had no sooner returned to her office when David came out of his. Alone.

"I'm going out to lunch with Alek, Tara. He's waiting in the car now. I probably won't be back for the rest of the day. You'll have to handle anything that

28

comes up." David's voice was completely normal, yet Tara felt herself grow warm at the speculative glance he passed over her.

"David, about this morning. I don't know how to explain, except—" She paused, searching for words, and David cut in gently. "Don't worry about it, Tara. You should know by now I'm broad-minded and anyway, Alek explained everything, even though it wasn't necessary. It's really none of my business. Now I've got to go, as we're meeting the contractor. See you tomorrow."

More confused than ever, Tara sat stunned. What in the name of sanity was going on? What explanation could Alek have given for his outrageous actions? And why wasn't it any of David's business? You would think a madman running around loose would be everybody's business.

The more she thought about it, the more convinced she became that Alek Rykovsky was playing some sort of cat-and-mouse game. But to what purpose? More than likely, she thought, his pride had been injured and he wanted to make her uncomfortable. Well! he was certainly succeeding there. But why involve David?

By the time the rose arrived Friday morning, she hardly gave the identity of its sender a second thought. After the events of the day before, it didn't seem to matter much. Besides, she had slept badly and was tired, not at all looking forward to round three with the Mad Russian. She was at a total loss as to what he hoped to gain, and so completely missed the clues.

It was a quiet weekend. Too quiet. Tara was not in the habit of running out several nights a week, but

29

she usually went out at least one night during the weekend. Sometimes with a man, but more often with a group of young friends, which included David and Sallie, for dinner or stay-at-home evenings of cards and conversation. This was the second weekend in a row she had not received a call or invitation from one of her friends, not even Sallie.

The only unusual thing that happened was on Saturday and Sunday morning when she went to the door to answer the bell only to find the hall empty except for the now familiar florist box containing a single white rose.

By Sunday night Tara decided the whole thing was very weird. She liked her quiet, but this was too much. Beginning to feel vaguely like the last person on earth, she reached for the phone with the intention of calling Sallie when its sudden jangling ring startled her so badly, she actually jumped.

"I didn't interrupt anything, did I, Tara?" Betsy's voice was as much of a surprise as her words, as Betsy seldom called and then usually only when she wanted something, as it seemed she did now.

"Interrupt anything? For heaven's sake, Betsy, it's after ten thirty. Tomorrow's a working day. I'll soon be going to bed." What kind of a wild existence did her sister think she lived, anyway?

"Well, Sis, you're such a close-mouthed thing, one never knows. Except of course, what one may read in the papers or"—she paused—"hear through the grapevine."

There was a definite insinuation on Betsy's last four words and Tara felt her skin prickle.

"What?"

"Doesn't matter. Look, Tara, the reason I called

30

was, if you decide to give up your apartment, will you let Ken and me know? Maybe even talk to your landlord for us?"

Give up her apartment? What in the world? Her tone was an equal mixture of exasperation and puzzlement. "Betsy, I don't know what you've heard or think, but—"

"Oh! I had no intentions of prying," Betsy interrupted, her words coming in a rush, tripping over each other. "I've told you how small Ken's place is and I thought I'd get my bid in if you were considering it. You know, I'm a big girl now and I'm hip to the ways of the world and I do understand. I mean, he's such a magnificent . . . fantastic hunk of man."

Skinny Kenny? Magnificent? Fantastic? Tara knew her sister was inclined to exaggerate, but this was too much. Puzzlement won out over exasperation. "Bets, I think some explanation is necessary," Tara began, only to have Betsy interrupt again.

"No, really, just keep us in mind. Okay? Bye." She hung up and Tara stared at the receiver in her hand as if she had never seen one before. Sighing deeply, she wondered if everyone around her was slipping over the edge, or if it was she who was going bananas.

A single white rose continued to arrive daily at the office, and by midweek Tara simply sniffed it appreciatively, stuck it in the vase, and went about her work. She was grateful for one thing: Aleksei Rykovsky hadn't shown up at the office at all and David treated her as if nothing had ever happened.

It was almost noon on Friday when Sallie dashed into the office. "Hi, Tara. Is David terribly busy? I

31

have something I want to check with him and I'm in an awful rush."

"David's never too busy to see you, Sallie." Tara laughed. "Go on in and surprise him."

In less than ten minutes Sallie was back, standing in front of her desk, pulling soft tan pigskin gloves over her hand.

"I wanted to check with him about the wine for tomorrow night. I was going to call him from home, but then Mother came to look after Tina, and I didn't think of it again until after I'd left the house." Sallie spoke quickly, glancing at the clock. "I'll miss you tomorrow night, Tara, but David explained everything and I do understand. At least I think I do." Sallie's expression held concern; she seemed almost hurt. "Oh, Lord! I have to run. I'm meeting Dave's mother for lunch and I'm going to be late." She grimaced, threw Tara a half-smile, and dashed out again.

Tara experienced the same prickling sensation in her skin she'd had the previous Sunday while talking to her sister, and with it a mild sense of alarm. What was this all about? It was beginning to seem that everyone understood everything but her. She was tempted to confront David but she could hardly go in and blurt out, "Why haven't you invited me to your party?"

She worried about Sallie's words and attitude the rest of the day and finally decided the only cause she could think of was Aleksei Rykovsky's extraordinary behavior the week before and her own unwilling involvement in it. But good Lord, she had been unwilling; surely they realized that. Then pride kept her from going in to question David.

As she left the office that afternoon, she hesitated

with a sudden aversion to spending the entire evening alone, confined within those few small rooms. Then with a quick, decisive step she walked to the car. Her mother's birthday was the following week and, as she had a sweet tooth that was rarely indulged, Tara decided to take a run to her favorite candy shop and buy her mother a large box of chocolates.

She turned onto Route 222 heading south and was past the consistory building before the beauty of the late October afternoon struck her. When she glanced at the grounds of Cedar Crest College to her right, her breath caught in her throat. The long fingers of the westering sun bathed the fall foliage in a golden glow, setting the russet leaves alight. The glory of the Pennsylvania autumn had always affected her with soul-wrenching intensity and today, caught so suddenly, the beauty of it all cut into her deeply. Hurt, confused by the events of the last few weeks, she was doubly vulnerable to the heart-twistingly beautiful power of nature.

She felt the hot sting of tears behind her eyes and shook her head impatiently. *This is ridiculous,* she thought moodily. The last few weeks she had spent most of her time either in her apartment or at the office. She needed a break, a diversion. She'd visit the gift shop on the floor above the candy shop, make herself a present of some small object. Hadn't she always heard that spending money on something not really needed could always lift a woman's spirits?

In the candy shop she gave her order to the clerk for the special assortment her mother loved, then slipped up the narrow stairway to the floor above. The gift shop was well stocked, the merchandise displayed on tables and shelves along the walls and down the center of the room, leaving a narrow aisle to walk around. Tara moved slowly, her eyes darting around, trying to see everything. Then her eyes stopped and focused on a painting on the wall. Studying the brilliant fall scene intently, she gave a sudden, startled "Oh" when a body jolted into her from behind.

"I'm terribly sorry," a pleasant male voice said close to her ear. "I'm afraid I wasn't watching where I was going."

She turned, mouth opened to reply but the words were never uttered for he exclaimed. "Tara! I don't know if you remember me. Craig Hartman, we met at David's six months ago."

Recognition brought a quick smile to her face. "Of course I remember. You're the young man who was getting ready to go to South America for your company."

"Right. I just got back on Tuesday. As a matter of fact I was going to call you as soon as I'd finished my report to the firm."

"Really?" she laughed. "Why?"

"To ask you to have dinner with me some evening." He grinned boyishly, and Tara remembered she'd liked this young man when first meeting him. "This is incredible seeing you here, of all places. What are you doing here?"

"Just browsing while I wait for a candy order to be packaged. And you?"

Again the boyish smile spread over his face. "I remembered late this afternoon that my sister's first wedding anniversary is tomorrow and dashed over here, after I left the office, for a gift. I was looking at the paintings and not watching where I was going when I bumped into you."

Tara grinned back. "And I was looking at one and didn't see you coming." She glanced back at the fall scene and his eyes followed hers. "That *is* nice," he murmured. "Are you going to buy it?"

"No," she laughed softly. "I'm afraid my budget wouldn't allow it."

"Then I think I will. Pat has a spot in her living room where it will go perfectly." He motioned to the sales clerk and asked her to wrap it up, then turned back to Tara. "Have dinner with me this evening," he said abruptly. "We can go from here. I know it's early, but we can have a drink or two first, get to know each other a little."

"But I haven't been home," she said, laughing in surprise. "I'm still in my work clothes."

His eyes went over her slowly, appreciatively, before he stated warmly: "You look lovely. Besides which, I've just come from work myself. What difference does it make? I'm sure they won't refuse to serve us."

They didn't, and over dinner she studied him unobtrusively. He wasn't much taller then she and, though slender, was compactly built. Fair, closely clipped curly hair complemented light blue eyes, and she though that although he didn't possess the devastating handsomeness of one Aleksei Rykovsky, he was certainly a very attractive man. Then she slid her eyes away with a flash of irritation at herself. What in the world had made her think of that miserable man, let alone make a comparison between him and Craig?

"Hey, there."

35

Tara looked up, startled and wide-eyed, at Craig's laughing voice. "I thought you'd dozed off for a minute. Not very good for my ego at all."

Tara laughed with him, firmly pushing the thought of the Mad Russian from her mind.

It was a pleasant evening. They laughed and talked for hours, discovering they had a few mutual friends besides David and Sallie.

When finally they said good night at the door of her apartment, Craig having followed her car in his own, she felt happier and more relaxed than she had in weeks.

Her lightened mood lasted through the weekend, even though the white rose appeared exactly as before, and the phone remained strangely silent.

She was walking to the filing cabinet early Monday afternoon when the phone rang and she stopped beside her desk to answer it. It was her mother, and she asked Tara, in an oddly strained voice, if they could have lunch together one day that week.

"Of course, Mama," she answered, a small wrinkle forming between her eyes at the strange tone of her mother's voice. "I'll tell you what. I was planning to take you shopping for your birthday present on Saturday. Why don't we wait, and I'll buy you lunch at Hess's?"

Her mother hesitated then agreed dully, and Tara felt a flicker of alarm. Was she not feeling well? Her mother loved the rare treat of having lunch at the large department store, famous for its sumptuous food, the large, luscious desserts, and her apparent disinterest now worried Tara.

"All right, Mama, I'll pick you up at nine thirty

Saturday morning. Okay?" Her mother agreed in the same strained tone, then said good-bye and hung up.

Her frown deepening, Tara lowered the receiver slowly as the office door opened behind her. A small shiver slithered up her spine, and the instrument clattered onto its cradle from nerveless fingers. She knew, somehow, who had come into the office and felt goose bumps tickle her upper arms moments before she felt his hand lift her hair and his lips touch her neck. She parted her lips but words wouldn't come. Shock, outrage, and something she didn't want to examine seemed to have frozen her mind and body.

His voice was a barely discernible murmur at her ear. "Have a good time Friday night, pansy eyes?"

She made a small, inarticulate sound in her throat, and he laughed softly, deeply before adding in a much stronger tone, "I've tried to stay away from this office, telling myself the nights should be enough, but it seems I've grown greedy and my self doesn't listen."

A shudder tore through her body at the caressing, loverlike tone, and she closed her eyes, willing him to go away. She felt David walk past them and go into his office, closing the door with a soft click, and her moan was a painful thing in her throat: "Oh, God!"

"Don't worry, darling," the fiend with the lover's voice whispered. "You'll understand everything very soon now, I'm afraid." Then he caught her rigid chin with his long fingers, turned her head, and brushed her mouth against his in a soft, tantalizing kiss before quickly releasing her and following David.

She was completely bewildered, feeling shattered and vaguely tearful.

The feeling remained throughout the week, and

she hardly noticed the white morning roses. One thing she did notice was the strange, speculative looks aimed at her from her co-workers in the front office. And that made her even more edgy and nervous.

CHAPTER THREE

By Saturday morning Tara had managed to pull herself together yet she still had to force a cheerful smile to her lips when she picked up her mother. The smile faded quickly at her first glimpse of her mother's face. Lines of strain pulled at the corners of her mouth, and she avoided Tara's eyes as she seated herself in the car.

As she drove downtown, Tara made a few vain attempts at conversation but finally gave up as the only responses she received were mumbled monosyllables.

They shopped a few hours, Tara becoming ever more concerned at her mother's lack of interest at everything they looked at. Finally, at eleven thirty, Tara gave up, saying gently, "Let's go have lunch now, Mama. Maybe we'll feel more like it after we've eaten."

She studied her mother during lunch, growing more uneasy by the minute. Her mother barely touched her food, and when they'd finished and were sipping their coffee, Tara asked anxiously, "Mama what's wrong? Aren't you feeling well?"

The eyes that Marlene Schmitt turned to Tara sent a shaft of pain to her heart, so reproachful and hurt was their expression.

"I'm sick at heart, Tara," her mother finally answered sadly. "So much so, I feel physically ill. After the way you talked to Betsy just three weeks ago, I can't believe you're doing this. And Tara, I can't bear it."

Tara's eyes widened at the pain in her mother's voice. What had she done to cause her mother this anguish?

"But Mama, what have I done?" Tara asked anxiously, watching with alarm her mother's eyes fill with tears.

"Oh, Tara, don't. I know I'm a little old-fashioned and naive, but I'm no fool."

"Mama, please—"

"No. I would listen to you, take your side, in most things. But not this." She paused, a sob catching in her throat, then went on, cutting off the defensive words on Tara's lips. "Your father asked—no, told—me to bring you back to the house. I must warn you, he is beside himself with anger."

The last word was no sooner out of her mother's mouth when Tara rushed into urgent speech.

"Mama, if you'll just ex—"

"Tara, please," her mother said softly, glancing around the crowded room. "I can't discuss this here. I won't talk here. I want to go home."

Tara sighed in frustration. "All right. Let's go and get it over with."

They drove home in silence, Marlene Schmitt quietly wiping the tears from her cheeks with a sodden tissue.

Tara bit her lip in vexation, frantically casting about in her mind for some transgression she may have committed to cause her mother such unhappiness.

She followed her mother into the house, her steps faltering as she entered the living room. They were all there. Her father, his face flushed a dark, angry red; Betsy; George; and even the fourteen-year-old Karl. Anger stirred, replacing some of her anxiety. *What in the world is this anyway?* she wondered. The words *kangaroo court* flashed into her mind, and she pushed the thought away. Good Lord! This was her family, not a band of enemies. Yet the atmosphere of censure was so thick, it touched her skin chillingly.

Ever defiant, the light of battle gleamed in Tara's eyes. She had no idea what this was all about but she'd be damned if she'd stand before those condemning eyes meekly. Her father's first words took the wind from her sails.

"Well, Tara. I'm surprised you have the nerve to face any of us after your big talk three weeks ago."

"Dad," Tara began patiently, "I haven't the vaguest idea what—"

"Haven't you?" Her father nearly choked on the words. "Haven't you just?" His eyes went around the room, touching every face, then settled again on Anyone else would have the sense to be ashamed, but Tara. "Look at her. Proud as a damned peacock. not our Tara. Oh, no. Rules were made for everyone else. Tara makes hers up as she goes along. You make me sick, girl."

"Herman—" his wife pleaded.

"Don't 'Herman' me. I've listened to you since she was a teen-ager. 'Tara's intelligent,' you said. 'She has good sense,' you said. 'She'll make us proud.' *Ha!* What she's doing is intelligent? Makes good sense? It's degrading, disgusting. I should have beat the rebellion out of her years ago."

The defiance in Tara's eyes had slowly changed to bewilderment. Never had she seen her father quite so angry. This was serious. Really serious. And she didn't have a clue as to what he was talking about.

"Dad, please. If you'll just explain—"

It seemed she was not to be allowed to speak, for he interrupted with a shouted, "Me explain? You think we're dumb Dutchmen, don't you? You think we're so stupid, we don't understand. You think your mother doesn't understand the gossip of her friends? You think your sister and brothers don't understand the behind-the-hand snickers of their friends? You think I don't understand the dirty remarks made by the men I work with?"

Tara wet her suddenly dry lips. Her fathers dark, mottled color frightened her, but his words frightened her more. This was more than serious; this was ugly. When she didn't reply at once, her father shouted, "Do you think we haven't heard of this man's reputation with women?"

Tara's head snapped up. *What man?* The silent question was answered loudly.

"Do you think we haven't heard how this rich Russian uses them and then kicks them aside? Oh, sure," he added, his voice dripping sarcasm. "He gives them anything they want. Anything, that is, except his name."

"You're wrong," Tara whispered, horrified.

"Of course." His sarcasm grew yet stronger. "That can't happen to you. You're too good for that." His eyes bored into her with hatred. "You've always thought yourself too good. Too good for us or this

42

house. Too good for the nice, hardworking young men who were interested in you. But not too good, apparently, to crawl into bed with that swine Rykovsky."

"Herman, don't." Tara heard her mother scream, but she couldn't help her. She could hardly breathe. Her father's words had hit her like a punch in the ribs, and she stood, white and trembling, staring at his face. Then she spun on her heel and ran, her mother's sobs beating on her ears.

Hours later, as she closed her apartment door behind her, she had no recollection of getting to her car. Or, for that matter, of driving up into the mountains. She had been brought to her senses by the long, blaring sound of the horn of the car she nearly ran head into. Shaken, sick to her stomach, face wet with tears she didn't even remember shedding, she slowed down the car then pulled in and stopped at the first observation parking area she came to. She hadn't left the car, as there were many tourists walking around, admiring the splendor of the panoramic view of the mountains, overlapping each other as if trying to push themselves forward in a proud display of their brilliant fall finery.

Tara sat still, hands gripping the steering wheel. Suddenly everything made sense. At least almost everything. Now she understood her sister's strange phone call two weeks ago. Now she understood David and Sallie's reserved attitude. And now she understood the sly looks of everyone in the office, the odd silence of her friends. They all thought she and Aleksei Rykovsky were—her mind shied from the word momentarily—*lovers*. The word pushed its way forward. They all thought he was her lover. Vivid

43

pictures followed the word into her mind and she gasped aloud. Seemingly of its own volition, her arm lifted her hand to her face and drew the back of it across her mouth then quickly turned to press cold fingers to slightly parted lips. She could actually feel his mouth against hers. Could feel again that confusing mixture of excitement and fear his lips had aroused. Her fingertips tingled and, lifting her hand, she stared at her fingers as if hypnotized. "Oh, God, no," she whispered.

Now she pushed herself away from the apartment door against which she'd slumped and stumbled across her living room and into the bedroom. Dropping her handbag and jacket onto the floor, she fell across the bed fully clothed, exhausted, her mind numbed into blankness. She had no idea how long she lay staring into space when the shrill ringing of the phone roused her. Dragging her body from the bed, she walked slowly to the living room, legs still shaking. Dropping heavily onto the chair by the phone, she picked up the receiver and said, dully, "Hello."

A pause, then Craig Hartman's voice came over the wire, hesitant, uncertain. "Tara?"

"Yes. . . . Craig?"

"I thought I had the wrong number," he laughed softly. "It didn't sound like you. Did you just get in?"

"Yes," she answered blankly. "But how did you know?"

"I rang your phone a couple of times this afternoon."

"Why?"

"To ask you to have dinner with me, silly. It's not too late. Will you come out with me?"

"Oh, Craig," she answered wearily. "Not tonight. I'm not feeling well."

He was instant concern. "I'm sorry. What's wrong?"

"Nothing serious. I have a blinding headache and I'm going to take some aspirin and go to bed."

"Sounds best. Hope you feel better tomorrow. May I call you one night next week?"

"Yes, any night. Thank you for inviting me."

"You bet! Take care of yourself. I'll call. Good night."

"Good night, Craig."

Tara replaced the receiver then sat staring at the white Princess phone, her brow knit in concentration. The numbness that had gripped her mind at the memory of Aleksei Rykovsky's kiss had been swept away, and her brain was asking questions.

What was his reputation with women? Tara had no idea. She seldom listened to that sort of gossip simply because she could not care less how other people conducted their private lives. What had her father said? Something about how he used women then tossed them aside. *Very probably true,* Tara thought, her lips curling slightly. The word *womanizer* seemed to fit in perfectly with *tyrant*—arrogant and bossy.

Aleksei Rykovsky's emerging character was an unsavory one. Yet not completely so, Tara admitted to herself grudgingly. His reputation concerning his work was excellent; this Tara knew. Not only from things David had said but also from what she'd observed herself.

According to David, whom Tara wouldn't dream of doubting, Alek was the most ethical businessman he'd ever met. The signing of a contract with Rykovsky, David had told her, was a mere formality. For, once given, his word was as binding as his signature. He managed his plant with a combination of rigid discipline and humane understanding. The finished product, before it left his plant, had to be of the highest quality. And his patience, when dealing either with other businessmen or his employees, was legend.

This last Tara had found a little hard to believe. She remembered vividly one afternoon in late August at the new plant site. She had gone with David to take notes as he conferred with Alek and the construction boss. It had been hot, the humidity hanging in the seventies. Tara had felt sticky and slightly headachy; the condition was not helped by the fact that Alek had been late, and they'd stood in the hot sun waiting for him. When he had finally arrived with a brief word of apology, Tara had felt her headache grow stronger at the sheer impact of his appearance.

Tara's eyes had run over him swiftly as he approached them. He had left his jacket in the car and Tara wet dry lips, watching the lithe movement of his body as he strode forward. Dark brown slacks hugged his slim hips and muscular thighs and his shirt clung damply to an alarmingly broad expanse of chest and shoulders. Deeply tanned arms contrasted strikingly with the creamy color of his short-sleeved shirt and the slim gold watch on his wrist. He still wore his tie but, in concession to the heat, he had pulled the knot loose and opened the two top buttons of his shirt. Frowning, Tara had shifted her eyes away with a flash of irritation at the blatantly sensual look of him. Not once, either then or since, had Tara considered the incongruity of her irritation: She had been on the site some twenty-five minutes and had not been an-

46

noyed by, or really even noticed, the fact that most of the workers were either bare-chested or had their shirts opened to the waist.

Other than a nod in her direction on arrival, Alek had seemed unaware of her existence while she stood beside David, pencil flying over her notepad. When the context of the discussion changed to that of not requiring note taking, Tara moved back and away a few feet to give the men privacy.

Flipping the pages as she checked over her notes, Tara had been only surfacely aware of the large, burly workman walking in her direction. As he moved to pass by, not much more than a foot in front of her, he stumbled and Tara glanced up with a startled "Oh!" Arms flailing the air as if to regain his balance, his one hand arced past her face and the next instant she went rigid as his large, grimy fingers clutched her right breast.

The subsequent action had the element of a film viewed from a speeded-up projector; and yet every movement remained clear in Tara's memory. Stepping back and away from those clutching fingers, Tara glanced in dismay at the soil mark on her otherwise pristine white sleeveless scooped-neck top. At the same time, from the moment the man had stumbled, Tara had peripherally seen Alek's head jerk up then had seen him moving, crossing the few feet of sun-baked yellow-brown earth in two long-legged strides. He reached the man at the same instant Tara stepped back, and her surprise changed to alarm as she saw his arm flash up then down, the edge of his hand striking a blow to the man's shoulder that drove him to his knees. Long hard fingers

47

strategically placed at the back of the man's neck kept him there.

"Are you trying to find out what it would be like to be paralyzed for the rest of your life?"

The tone of Alek's voice had sent a shuddering chill through Tara's body. Icy, deadly, his words hung like a pall on the suddenly still, hot air. Tara became aware of the work stoppage of the men in their vicinity, the intent look of attention on the men's faces, including David and the construction boss.

The burly workman at Alek's feet gave a strangled sound in the negative, and Alek's hand moved from the back of his neck.

"If you, or any other member of this work crew, ever make an advance on Mr. Jennings's secretary again, you'll find out pretty damned quickly, so pass the word. Now get the hell away from here and get back to work."

For such a large man, the worker was on his feet and moving away at what Tara was sure was a record pace.

She had very little time to observe the man's retreat, for Alek's eyes, blazing with blue fury, were turned on her. Swiftly they raked the upper part of her body then returned to bore into hers. His voice a harsh whisper, he snapped, "As for you, Miss Schmitt, may I suggest that in the future you dress with a little more decorum when you're on the site. Unless, of course, you enjoy this kind of attention."

With that he turned and walked back to David. Shocked, Tara stood open-mouthed, staring at his back. Shock was at once replaced by humiliation and anger at what she considered his unwarranted attack on both herself and the hapless workman. That his last whispered words had obviously reached no other ears but her own was little consolation.

Turning, cheeks red with embarrassment, Tara spun around and stalked to David's car, slamming the door after sliding onto the front seat. *That arrogant, obnoxious brute,* she raged silently. Where did he get off speaking to her like that? Dress with more decorum indeed! Her clothes were perfectly decent. Moreover, they were in perfectly good taste.

Honest in his business dealings, he may be, Tara thought. *Fanatical in his demand for quality work, perhaps. But patient? Hardly.*

Now, still sitting next to the phone, Tara wondered about his supposed reputation with women. With a manner as abrasive as his, how in the world had he acquired it? No woman playing with all fifty-two of her cards would care to get within shouting distance, let alone close enough to be used then tossed aside. . . .

Her stomach gave a protestingly empty growl, startling her out of her thoughts. She had overslept this morning and had gulped a half glass of orange juice for breakfast. Tara had barely picked at her lunch and now at—she glanced at her watch—eight fifteen her body was sending out a cry for nourishment.

Like an automaton she stood up and walked into the kitchen; she started a pot of coffee, put an egg in the poacher, and dropped two pieces of bread in the toaster. A few minutes later, as she munched her egg and toast thoughtfully, her mind went back to the question: *Who had perpetrated a rumor of this kind? Why would someone want to? And equally baffling,*

49

how? She had seen the man only four times in three weeks. Three times in the office, and then only briefly, and that one time here at her own apartment. Surely not even the most imaginative person could make anything of a twenty-minute visit. And no one had witnessed those incidents in the office except David. David? Tara shook her head firmly. David would have told no one but Sallie, and Sallie, Tara was positive, would not repeat it. But then who? and why? and dammit, how?

Tara got up, walked to the counter, and refilled her coffee cup. As she turned back to the table, she became still with an altogether new thought. *Her* name and reputation were not the only ones involved here. Had word of this reached Aleksei Rykovsky's ears? She somehow felt certain that it had. He was not the man to miss anything. Whatever must he be thinking?

The phone's ringing broke her thoughts, and she went to answer it, carrying her coffee with her.

"Hello."

"Tara, it's me, Betsy." *As if I wouldn't know,* Tara thought wryly. "Look, Sis, I just wanted you to know I don't feel the same as Dad does."

"About what?" Tara asked, tiredly.

"Oh, you know," her sister snorted impatiently. "About you and him. I think you would have been dumb not to grab him, he's so handsome and rich."

Tara was quiet so long digesting the greedy sound and intent of her sister's words that Betsy said sharply, "Tara?"

"Good-bye, Betsy." Tara pressed her finger on the disconnect button on the inside of the receiver then carefully placed it on the table next to the cradle. She certainly didn't need any more calls or opinions like that tonight.

Sipping at her still hot coffee, she turned to go back to the kitchen when the door chime rang. *Oh, now what?* she thought balefully. Staring at the door, she considered not answering, when it chimed again.

Sighing deeply, she walked across the pale beige carpet, unlocked the door, pulled it open, and froze. Cool and relaxed, Alek Rykovsky stood in the hall, his hands jammed in the pockets of his black raincoat. *Was it raining?* Tara wondered irrelevantly. *Must be,* she decided, noting the damp spots on his wide shoulders. His coat hung open and he looked trim and muscular in the close-fitting, black brushed-denim jeans and a white turtleneck bulky knit sweater. *He was one unnerving sight,* Tara admitted ruefully to herself. If someone had to smear her name in connection with a man, at least whoever it was had chosen a handsome devil.

"May I come in?" he asked pointedly. "Or are you going to just stand there looking daggers at me?"

She jerked her eyes away, feeling her face go hot. Embarrassment put a sharp edge to her tongue.

"Come in if you must," she said cuttingly, pulling the door wider. Perfectly shaped lips twitching, he strolled past her, and in agitation she slammed the door shut. Lifting her cup to her lips, she took a long, calming sip.

"I'd like some of that." He nodded at her cup.

Turning abruptly, she marched into the kitchen with Alek right on her heels. She went to the counter, snatched a mug from its peg on the mug tree, filled it to the brim, then turned and gave an exclaimed "Oh," not having realized he was still close behind

51

her. Some of the hot liquid splashed over the side of the cup and onto her hand, and he snatched the cup away from her with a growled "What the hell are you trying to do? Scald yourself?"

"I—I—didn't know you were so close," she stammered.

The fires that had momentarily lit his eyes were banked into a bright glitter. "Do I frighten you, Tara?" he chided.

"No, of course not," she snapped. "You startled me, that's all." She turned to refill her own cup, trying in vain to control her shaking hands.

"Hmmm," he murmured judiciously, shrugging out of his raincoat. He draped the coat over the back of a kitchen chair, picked up his cup and drank from it, then, one dark brow arched questioningly, said, "You seem upset about something. Anything wrong?"

Something about his too casual tone annoyed her and, her voice oversweet, she purred, "Have you heard the latest gossip?"

"About us?" he replied, his tone equally sweet.

Anger flared fiercely, and her usually soft brown eyes flashed. "No, the Prince of Wales," she spat. "Of course about us."

He nodded, watching her mounting anger solemnly.

"Who would do something like this," she burst out angrily.

"Don't you know?"

She jerked her head up to stare at him, suspecting some sort of condemnation. His face was expressionless, his eyes coolly calculating. "No, I don't know! I can't believe for a minute that any of my friends would spread such a vicious story."

"The idea of you and me together is vicious?"

Tara eyed him stormily, hating the theatrically affronted tone of his voice. "You may be amused, Mr. Rykovsky. This kind of thing enhances a man's aura. But my reputation is ruined."

"Is that so very important today?" he asked dryly.

"Of course it is," she cried.

"Well, you may have a point," he murmured. "Come to think of it, you're right."

"What do you mean?"

He drained his cup, walked to the sink, rinsed it, and placed it in the draining rack. Then he turned, took her cup from her hand, and did the same to it before asking, "Wouldn't we be more comfortable in the living room?" Not waiting for an answer, he scooped up his coat and strode out of the kitchen.

Gritting her teeth, Tara followed him, entering the living room in time to see him drop into a chair and stretch his long legs out comfortably.

"If you're sure you're comfortable, Mr. Rykovsky, perhaps you'd explain what you said before."

"What was that?" he asked innocently, then smiled sardonically. "Oh, yes, about your being right. Well, you see, Tara, for all our big talk of equal rights, I'm afraid a great many of us men are still dreadfully chauvinistic. Most will jump happily into bed with any 'liberated' woman who'll have him. But, and it's a very big *but,* these very same men, when they finally decide they are ready to get married, will look around for a relatively untouched woman. I say relatively untouched because even the most naive of us are aware that today there are not really that many virginal women over the age of twenty. So you see, it's the old double standard. While he wants to bed as many as possible, he wants to marry an untouched one. Deplorable perhaps, but nonetheless true. It's the nature of the beast."

As he spoke, Tara felt her anger grow apace with her embarrassment. Now, pink-cheeked, eyes snapping, she jumped up out of her chair.

"Beast is right. How grossly unjust that attitude is."

"That goes without saying. But then, who ever said that life was just?"

He stood up slowly, lazily uncoiling like a large, dark cat. Tara walked across the room to the window facing the street, suddenly, unaccountably, nervous.

"I don't know what to do about this," she almost whispered. "My family's upset. My friends have made themselves scarce. Incredibly, in this day and age, I feel ostracized."

"You have one option that would stop the talk at once." He spoke quietly, his eyes keen on her face as she turned to look questioningly at him.

"Accept my proposal. Marry me." He walked slowly to her and she felt her heart begin to thud frantically, her legs tremble.

Hoping to stop his determined movement toward her, she sneered. "You mean you're unlike other men? You're willing to saddle yourself with a—what is the word—*tainted* woman?"

He laughed low in his throat, the sound slipping down her spine on tiny, icy feet.

"As I'm supposed to be the man who 'tainted' you, I can't see that it makes any difference."

He stopped in front of her, reaching up to touch her silvery hair, gleaming in the soft glow of the table lamp beside her.

"Such fantastic hair," he murmured. "I want to see it fanned out on a pillow under me, Tara." He pinched a few strands between thumb and forefinger and drew his hand down its long length. "I want to bind myself in it like a silken net." Tara felt the serpent of excitement uncoil in her midriff as he brought the strands to his lips. "I want to draw it across your beautiful mouth and kiss you breathless through it." In unwilling fascination she watched his eyes darken, narrow with desire; felt his hand slide to her nape; felt long fingers curl into the soft thickness and draw her face to his. His mouth a breath away from hers, he whispered hoarsely, "Marry me, Tara." Then he covered her trembling lips with his hard, firm ones in an urgent, demanding kiss.

Tara stiffened, fighting the insidious languor that invaded her body as if fighting for her life. She had been kissed many times but never had she felt like this. Her veins seemed to be flowing with liquid fire that burned and seared and ate up her resistance. His hands moved down her spine, then gripped convulsively, flattening her against the long, hard length of his body. She felt dizzy, light-headed, barely able to hear the small voice of reason that cried, *Step back,* when all she wanted was to get closer, closer. His hand moved up and under her knit top, and she shivered deliciously at the feel of his fingers on her bare skin. The voice of reason broke through when his hand moved over her breast possessively. Using her last remaining dregs of will, she tore her mouth from his and spun out and away from his arms, sobbing, "No. No. No."

He didn't come after her but stood studying her pale, frightened face intently, breathing deeply to regain control.

"You're a fool, Tara," he finally said, his voice

55

calm, devoid of inflection. "I could give you every-thing you ever wanted. And you are not indifferent to me. I've just proven that."

Tara stood rigid, forcing herself to meet the hard, blue glitter of his eyes. Hands clenched into fists to keep from trembling, she wondered, in a vague panic, why she'd felt chilled to the bone since spinning out of his arms. Then fatigue struck; suddenly her shoulders drooped, and she felt sick to tears, the events of this horribly long day pressing down on her. She turned from him to stare sightlessly through the window and said, wearily, "Go away."

She didn't see the swift flash of concern in his eyes and when she turned back to him, it was gone.

"The offer will stay open, Tara, if you change your mind." His eyes raked her, noting her pallor, the blue smudges of tiredness under her eyes. He took one step toward her, and she cried out, "Will you please go and leave me alone. Mr. Rykovsky, please."

"Since we're supposedly sleeping together, don't you think you could call me Alek," he chided gently.

Her head dropped and her voice was a tired, ragged whisper. "Alek, please, please go."

Her chin was lifted by one long finger and she found herself gazing into surprisingly gentle blue eyes. His mouth brushed hers lightly. "You're ex-hausted, pansy eyes. Stay in bed tomorrow and think about me. Lock up after me." Again his lips brushed hers, then he whispered, "Good night, lover, for whether you think so now or not, I am going to be your lover."

Then he moved swiftly across the room, snatching up his raincoat without pausing, and went through the door, closing it softly.

Tara stared after him, tears running down her face, feeling unaccountably abandoned. Too tired to probe her emotions or even think, she walked across the room and locked the door as commanded. And it had been a command. Then she turned off the lights and went to her bedroom, leaving the phone off the hook.

CHAPTER FOUR

Sunday was a short day, as Tara slept past noon. She woke with a dull headache and equally dull senses and moved about the apartment like a pale, uninterested wraith. What could she do to combat the rumors being spread connecting her name with Alek's? What could she do when she didn't even know the source of those rumors? And could she really do anything if she did know the source? A charge of slander has to be proved, and even if she could prove it, did she want that kind of publicity? The questions tormented her all day and by early evening had turned her dull headache into a piercing throb. At nine thirty, feeling half sick to her stomach, she gave it up and went to bed.

Nine hours of deep, uninterrupted sleep did wonders for her. Rested and refreshed, her headache gone, she faced Monday morning unflinchingly. She dressed extra carefully in a white long-sleeved silk shirt; black, gray, and white plaid skirt; black vest, the front panels embroidered in white-silk thread; and three-inch narrow-heeled gray suede boots to the knee. Topping the outfit off with a belted, black suede jacket that made her silver-blond hair look almost white, she slung her gray shoulder bag over her arm and swung out of the apartment fighting fit.

The long, careful look and silent whistle of appreciation she received from David when he entered the office boosted her morale even more. The smile she bestowed on him was breathtaking and the most natural David had seen in over a week. He stared bemusedly at her then grinned back and headed for his own office, pausing in the doorway to say, "Ask Terry Connors to come to my office, please."

Tara nodded, lifted the phone, punched the interoffice button, and waited for Connie Delp, the front-office typist, to answer.

A few minutes later Terry sauntered into her office for all the world like he owned the building. "Morning, beautiful, how's tricks?"

The words themselves were innocuous but the suggestive twist to his lips lent them a meaning that sent a cold stab of fear through her midsection. She had no time to question him, however, as he went straight through to David's office.

She sat pondering his words a few seconds, then gave herself a mental shake. She was getting hyper over all this, for heaven's sake; if she wasn't careful, she'd soon be reading double meanings into everything anyone said to her. In annoyance she turned back to her work, soon forgetting the incident.

An hour and a half later Terry left David's office and stopped at her desk. Glancing up questioningly, Tara caught the same twisted smile on his face before he sobered and said softly, "How about having dinner with me some time?"

Tara felt her scalp tingle in premonition, but she

managed to keep her voice level. "I told you before that I won't go out with you, Terry."

"Yeah, but that was then and now is now." His smile was an insinuation that made her skin crawl.

"Nothing has happened to change my mind," she said evenly.

"Oh, I don't expect you to two-time him. Not many women have that kind of guts. But when he's through with you—and with his track record it won't be too long—maybe you'll be glad of an invitation out."

While he was speaking, Tara felt her nerves tighten, her fingers grip the edge of her typewriter. With effort she kept her voice cool. "I don't know what you're talking about."

"Come off it, sweetheart," he jeered. "Everyone knows."

He grinned at her crookedly, his head tilted to one side, then he gave a short, nasty laugh. "You're cool as well as beautiful, baby, and I can see what he wants with you, but you can stow the innocent act. Hell, he may as well have taken an ad in the paper." He waved his hand at the bud vase on the corner of her desk. "The roses, the few—how should I say it?—'polite' inquiries he made about you months ago. His car parked in front of your apartment all night— every night—only confirmed everyone's suspicions." Again he gave that nasty laugh. "He even spoke to me one morning as I was on my way to work, after he'd left your apartment."

He stood a moment studying her stricken, wide-eyed face, then snorted, "I told you to can the act, kid. You may think we're a bunch of idiots, but even us peasants can add one and one and come up with two. You must have something special, seeing as how he comes to you rather than move you into his building, the way he usually does with his mistresses."

Tara had been staring in unseeing disbelief, but at his last words her vision cleared and focused on his leering face.

"Get out of my office," she said through clenched teeth, "before I call David and tell him you're annoying me."

"You win, sweetheart," Terry sneered. "But just remember who your friends are after he's through with you." He walked to the door then paused with his hand on the knob and shot over his shoulder, "I mean when the lesser males start calling, more than happy to sample the big man's leavings." On the last word he stepped through the doorway and closed the door with a sharp click.

White-faced, trembling, an odd buzzing sound in her head, Tara stared at the door, devoid, for the moment, of all feeling.

"Aleksei Rykovsky!"

The two words, murmured in a harsh whisper, sounded more like a bitter curse than a man's name. Following the words, which caused actual physical pain, white-hot anger tore through her mind; cleansing anger, motivating anger that unlocked the frozen state she'd been in and set her mind in action. She still had no idea why but now she knew how and, most importantly, who.

With careful, deliberate movement Tara pressed the intercom button and said coolly, "David, I'm sorry but I must leave the office for a short time. I have an appointment."

David, his tone indicating he was deeply immersed in his work, answered unconcernedly, "Okay, Tara, have Connie pick up on any incoming calls and take as long as you like."

"Thank you."

Tara relayed the instruction to Connie, then, her every movement still careful and deliberate, she covered her typewriter, slipped her arms into her jacket, removed her handbag from her bottom desk drawer, plucked the white rose from the bud vase and dropped it into her wastebasket, and left the office. She was going scalp-hunting.

It was less than a twenty-minute drive from David's office to Alek's large, antiquated machine shop. Tara used those minutes to put together the pieces of this bizarre puzzle. His words of Saturday night came as clearly as if he were sitting next to her in the car and had just spoken them.

"Don't you know?"

She had thought, then, that he was in some way accusing her of keeping information from him. Now she realized he had been probing to ascertain if she had any suspicions of him.

She went over and over the whole sordid mess and decided, not for the first time, that this man was not quite on-center; something was twisted inside. If it hadn't been for the anger that had resolved itself into a cold, hard fury, she might have been afraid of what she was about to do.

Alek's offices were located on the second floor of the sprawling old building. As Tara mounted the narrow staircase, she stiffened her spine in preparation to do battle. Steps evenly paced, firm, she walked along the long narrow hallway, glancing at closed doors marked PERSONNEL, SALES, and ACCOUNTING until finally reaching what she knew was her destination, the very last door, marked PRIVATE.

Gripping the knob, she drew a deep breath and walked in. The woman sitting at a desk some five feet inside the door was about thirty with a calm, withdrawn face and cool, intelligent eyes.

"May I help you?"

The impersonal smile and well modulated tones were the epitome of the superefficient secretary. No slouch in that department herself, Tara matched exactly her tone and manner.

"Yes, I would like to see Mr. Rykovsky, please. If it's convenient."

The cool eyes flickered with a degree of respect. "You have an appointment?"

Tara's lips twitched in wry amusement. This paragon knew damned well she had no appointment.

"No I haven't, but if he is not too busy, I'd appreciate a few minutes. It is rather important."

"I see," judiciously. "If you'll have a seat, I'll inquire, Miss . . . ?"

"Schmitt. Tara Schmitt."

She was left to cool her heels some fifteen minutes before that impersonal voice said, "Mr. Rykovsky will see you now, Miss Schmitt."

Tara's heels may have cooled, but her emotions were still at flash point, although this was not revealed as she rose gracefully to her feet, her outward appearance under rigid control.

"Thank you." Her voice a quiet murmur, she stepped past the secretary, who held open the door, and into the large room, seemingly dwarfed by the overwhelmingly masculine presence of its owner.

"Good morning, Tara." His low, silky voice slid

over her, setting her teeth on edge. "You're looking exceptionally beautiful this morning."

And he is looking exceptionally handsome, she thought bitterly. Dressed in an obviously expensive, perfectly tailored charcoal-gray vested suit, complemented by a pearl-gray silk shirt and oyster-white tie, the effect of him on the senses was devastating. *How could it be,* Tara wondered, *that someone could appear so shatteringly good on the outside and be so thoroughly rotten on the inside?*

She watched his eyes grow sharp when, without speaking, she stood studying him, even though the voice remained smooth.

"Sit down, Tara."

"I prefer to stand, Mr. Rykovsky."

"Mr. Rykovsky? Saturday night it was Alek." The voice was still smooth but beginning to show awareness of things being not quite right.

"Saturday night I was still an ignorant, innocent fool," she stated coldly.

One dark eyebrow arched fleetingly; the voice matched the eyes in sharpness. "You're upset. What's happened?"

"Upset?" she cried. "Upset? You set out with a deliberate intent to ruin my reputation then dare to stand there calmly and say I'm upset? No, *Mister* Rykovsky, I am not upset. I am red-hot furious."

His face went suddenly expressionless; his narrowed eyes went wary as he watched the pink flares of angry color tinge her cheeks, her soft brown eyes flash.

"All right," he said evenly. "You know. Now sit down and calm yourself, and we'll discuss it."

Eyes wide in astonishment, she nearly choked.

"Calm myself? I don't want to calm myself. And I don't want to discuss it. What I want is an explanation for what you've done and—" The sound of her voice, beginning to rise sharply, made her check her words. Breathing deeply, trying to regain control, she glared at him across the few feet of deep-pile carpeting that separated them.

"Tara"—his gentle voice tried to soothe—"if you'll calm—"

She didn't let him finish. Fighting to regain control, nails gouging into her palms, she ground out: "Were you bored? Was this your perverted idea of a joke? A way to break up a dull time in your life? Well, I don't think you're funny. I think you're sick. You need your head ex—"

"Tara." The silky voice had taken on a decidedly serrated edge, then smoothed out again. "That's enough. Now be quiet and listen a minute. If you let yourself think, you'll know why I did it. I told you twice. It was no joke, and I was not trying to be funny. Also I'm not sick. I simply know what I want and I am not afraid to go after it."

"No matter what method you use," she gasped. "Or who gets hurt?"

"I admit, in this instance, my methods were a bit unorthodox, but really, Tara, you're not all that injured. Good grief, woman, do you really think, today, that anyone gives a damn who is sleeping with who?"

He had remained so imperturbable, so unaffected through this incredible interview, that Tara was gripped with the urge to scream at him.

"My family gives a damn. *You* don't have to watch my mother cry or face my father's anger."

"That's right, I don't," he stated firmly. "But I will

if you give the word. Say you'll marry me, and I'll be at your parents' door within the hour to pacify them."

Tara was beginning to feel as if she'd stepped into some sort of unreal world, a fantasy land. *Things like this just don't happen,* she thought. Shaking her head as if to clear her mind, she said, haltingly, "I don't understand. I'm sure there must be any number of eager females ready and willing to comply with your slightest whim. Why have you singled me out to torment?"

His face hardened and a muscle rippled at the corner of his tautened jawline. "You're right. There are a number of females ready and willing." His eyes, searing like twin blue flames, raked her body boldly, heightening her color still more with embarrassment. "But, for some reason, my body demands the possession of yours. It is as simple as that. I want you. I intend having you."

Eyes wide in disbelief, she stared at him several seconds. The self-assurance, the powerful drive, the pure, unadulterated arrogance of this man was beyond her comprehension. Throat dry, she whispered, "My father was right. You are a swine."

"No name-calling, Tara." The tone gave a soft warning.

Beyond the point of heeding any warning, soft or firm, she laughed cynically. "Name-calling? I couldn't force past my lips the names I'd like to call you." Tears of anger, frustration, bitterness, blurred her eyes. Grimly she added, "You, in your exalted position of the male, may think that today no one really gives a damn. But then you didn't have to stand and listen to your father, in so many words, call you a

66

wh-whore." Her throat had closed, and she barely managed to get the last word out. Gulping air quickly, she stifled a sob, saying, "You don't have to listen to the snickering innuendos of the people in your office or the dirty suggestions of Terry Conners."

"Tara!"

Alek had remained standing behind his desk from the time she'd entered his office almost an hour ago. Now, moving with the lithe swiftness of a large mountain cat, he was around the desk and in front of her, his long-fingered hands grasping her shoulders painfully.

"I'll kill him," he snarled.

"And my father?" she cried wildly. "And every other man who'll think I'm fair game from now on?"

"Stop it," he commanded harshly, giving her a hard shake.

It was the last straw. All the fight went out of her and the tears that had been threatening for the last five minutes overflowed and ran down her flushed cheeks. Emotionally strung out, she suddenly felt too tired to care anymore and she stood, dimly studying the faintly embossed pattern on his tie. The pattern swirled and swam and she closed her eyes. She heard him sigh deeply, felt his hands loosen their hold on her shoulders, slide around her back. She felt the muscles and sinews in his arms tighten as he gathered her close. A strange feeling of being safe, protected, blanketed her numbed mind. Wearily, she rested her forehead against the hard wall that was his chest and, crying freely, released the misery that gripped her throat.

"Tara . . . don't."

The harsh tone of a moment ago had been replaced by a soft entreaty. He lowered his head over hers in yet another strangely protective gesture, and she felt his lips move against her hair. His head lowered again and now, his lips close to her ear, his words penetrated the mistiness.

"Dusha moya, Tara, *ya te lyoob-lyoo."*

He'd said those same strange words once before, yet it wouldn't be till much later that she'd wonder about their meaning. For now the words had a somehow soothing effect, and she shivered as a momentary peace enveloped her.

Vaguely she became aware of a tiny, nagging voice that told her that she should not be inside the warm, protective circle of his arms. But it felt so right, as if she belonged there more than anywhere else in the world. In the effort to silence that tiny, insistent voice, she turned her head and felt her slightly parted lips make contact with his taut, rough jaw. In bemusement she heard his sharply indrawn breath.

"Don't cry, pansy eyes. Nothing on this earth is worth your tears."

His tone, more than his words, was a gentle seducement. Warm, liquid gold flowed over and through her, seeming to enclose the two of them in a soft, golden world of their own. Without conscious thought her hands slid inside his jacket and she felt vague resentment against the material of his vest and shirt that denied her fingers the feel of his skin.

At her touch he went still, then his one hand moved up and under her hair, fingers spreading, to cradle her head. Slowly he turned her face to his, his lips brushing her cheek lightly, his breath tickling her eyelashes. Time seemed suspended inside that golden circle, and with a soft sigh Tara relaxed, allowing her arms to slide around his waist.

"I shouldn't be here," she murmured, forgetting and not caring, for the moment, why.

"You shouldn't be anywhere else. You belong exactly where you are." *Soft, his tone is so soft,* she thought. It was an inducement that drew her farther into that magic circle.

"Tara."

A hoarsely whispered groan, and then his mouth covered hers, gently, sweetly silencing that tiny nagging voice of reason.

His kiss was a tender exploration of her mouth, making no demands, asking nothing of her. At first she lay passive in his arms, her bruised emotions soothed by the glow of contentment stealing through her. But ever receptive to gentleness, tenderness, she was soon responding, her lips making an exploration of their own.

The kiss seemed to go on forever and ended much too soon. She murmured a soft protest when his mouth left hers and buried her face in the curve of his shoulder. Light as snowflakes, his lips touched her closed eyelids then moved to rest against her temple. Strong fingers gently massaged the back of her neck and for a few seconds Tara drifted in a gold-hued void that knew no thought or pain.

His words broke the golden spell, allowing the tiny voice to become a shout. "You're getting yourself upset over this, Tara, when it could be settled so simply by marrying me."

What do you think you're doing? the now shrill voice of her conscience demanded. *What happened to that sense of outrage that filled you on hearing Terry*

Conners's words? What about the fine, bright flame of fury that propelled you to this confrontation? A feeling of intense self-betrayal shot through her and she shuddered in self-disgust.

Alek misinterpreted her shudder as a sign of surrender, and he murmured, "Well, Tara?"

Tara drew a deep breath, took one step back, and pushed her hands hard against his chest. Unprepared for her action, his hold broke, and she was free of the reason-destroying circle of his arms.

Turning quickly, she ran for the door, her hand groping for the knob. Flinging the door open, shame and guilt strangling her throat, she whispered "No" to his commanded, "Tara, wait."

Blindly, she ran past his wide-eyed, incredulous secretary, along the hall, down the narrow stairway, and out the entrance door as if a pack of wild dogs were snapping at her ankles.

Trembling almost uncontrollably, she drove straight to her apartment with one thought pounding in her head. *Get home, be safe. Get home, be safe.*

Still running, she dashed up the steps and along the short hall to her apartment. Gasping for breath, she unlocked the door; dashed inside, slammed it shut, double-locked it, and leaned back against it.

On shaky legs she stumbled across the room and dropped onto the sofa. What in the sweet world was the matter with her? Never had she experienced this cloying, panicky feeling. She felt her throat close; then her eyes filled and with a murmured "Oh, Lord," her body fell sideways onto the cushions and she was crying, sobbing like a child, hurt, alone, lost.

For over an hour Tara lay in a crumbled heap, the wracking sobs and tears slowly dwindling to sniffles

70

and an occasional hiccup. Gradually awareness crept back and with a sigh she pushed herself upright. She had to call David.

David's voice was a reassuringly normal sound in a world gone suddenly very abnormal.

"I'm sorry, David," she sniffed, "but I won't be back today, I'm not feeling well."

Instant concern colored David's warm voice. "What's wrong, Tara?" A short pause, then: "Honey, have you been crying?"

"No, no," she reassured hastily. "I think I've had a sudden allergic reaction to something. I've been sneezing like mad and my eyes have been watering and I look a mess." *Well,* she thought, grimacing, *the last part's true.*

"Are you sure?" He sounded skeptical. "What could have brought this on?"

Tara cast about frantically and grabbed at the first thing that came to mind. "I'm not sure, but I think it must be the roses I've had on my desk the last few weeks." *Would he buy it?* she wondered. He did.

"More than likely. Have you seen a doctor?"

"No. I—I don't think that's necessary. I'll take an allergy capsule."

"Well, if it doesn't help you get better by tomorrow morning, get yourself to a doctor. Don't worry about the office but call me and let me know how you feel."

"All right, David, I will. And thank you."

"For what?" he snorted, then warned. "Now take care, Tara, I mean it."

"Yes, sir," came the meek reply. "Oh, and David, would you do something for me?"

"Anything I can."

"Would you call and stop delivery on the roses?

The name of the florist is on the box in my waste-basket."

"Sure thing, honey. Be good and get well."

He hung up. Tara smiled gently as she replaced the receiver. David hated saying good-bye and so he never did.

Speaking with David had restored her equilibrium somewhat, and with a firmer tread she went to the kitchen and brewed a pot of coffee. While the coffee perked away happily, she made herself half a sandwich and ate it in grim determination. When the electric pot shut itself off, she placed the pot, a small jug of milk, and a mug on a tray and returned to the living room.

Sitting with the mug of the steaming brew cradled in her hands, she turned her mind to her recent encounter and the events that led to it. She still found it incredible, if not completely unbelievable, that anyone would go to such lengths to amuse himself. In her book, that constituted a pretty weird sense of humor.

"It was no joke, and I was not trying to be funny."

His words slithered through her mind, and she shivered violently.

"Garbage." She said the word aloud and then repeated it silently. *Garbage.* Everything he'd said was exactly that. So much garbage. How she longed to make him pay for what he'd done to her. But how? Reluctantly she admitted to herself that chances of her hurting him in some way were practically nil.

As were her chances of repairing the damage he'd done. How did one combat nebulous hints? Innuendo? Veiled suggestions? She could go to her family and her closest friends and explain exactly what had happened, but would they believe it? Would she if she heard a story like that from someone? Not likely. Oh, yes, he'd been clever. Very clever. So what could she do? Move away? Where? And was it worth it? As he'd suggested, speculation, talk, couldn't cause her any lasting pain. *But he could,* an insidious voice whispered deep in her mind.

In sudden renewed fear, almost panic, she argued with the errant thought. How could he hurt her anymore? She didn't care what he said or did. Wouldn't care if he dropped dead tonight. The sudden twist of pain that clutched at her heart shocked her.

Frantically she moved about, refilling her coffee cup, walking to the TV to switch it on, anything to still those silly thoughts and emotions.

She watched a few minutes of the news then, much calmer, she decided her only course of action was to put on a bright face and brazen it out. In time the talk would die down, become a ninety-day wonder, and in due time she'd be able to forget it—and him.

But will you? that small, perverse voice demanded.

CHAPTER FIVE

The following two days went fairly well. She breezed into the office as usual, gave Terry a frosty smile as usual, talked a few minutes with Jeannie at coffee-break time, and breathed a heartfelt sigh of relief that the roses had stopped being delivered. Chalk one up for her.

On Tuesday evening she'd crept outside and scanned the street for his car. There it was, bold as brass, and it left a somewhat brassy taste in her mouth. Where the devil did the miserable man go after he parked it there? Back in her apartment she pondered on what, if anything, she could do about its presence. Should she call the police and report it as abandoned? And if they checked the license number and found out who it belonged to, then what? Alek Rykovsky was a respected businessman. If asked why his car was parked there, he could say he'd been visiting friends or had lent it to a friend in the neighborhood and he'd be believed without further question. And where would that leave her? Looking pretty damned silly. With reluctance she told herself: *Ignore the car.*

Wednesday moved along as Tuesday had, and she was beginning to think she'd get through this mess with some degree of composure. She even had an added bonus discovering Alek's car among the missing. Then the bottom fell out. Craig called. His first words jarred her out of her complacency.

"Look, Tara, I know you're alone because I happen to know Rykovsky's at a testimonial dinner tonight."

"Craig, I—"

"No, don't bother to explain. I understand. The only thing that makes me mad is that you didn't tell me the night we had dinner together. He sure as hell isn't trying to keep it a secret. If you'd told me, I wouldn't have built up any hopes. And I had."

"Craig, please, let me explain."

"Not necessary. You owe me nothing. But look, Tara, if anything happens, I mean, if you split or anything and need a shoulder to cry on, call me, will you?"

Why bother? Why even bother to explain to people who just wouldn't listen, or wouldn't believe it if they did?

"Yes, Craig," she answered softly, a wealth of defeat in her voice.

She went to bed depressed and woke the same way, but plastered a determined smile on her face anyway.

The morning went by without a hitch, and her spirits lifted. In an attempt to keep them up Tara decided to leave the office at lunchtime and treat herself to a fattening lunch of lasagna at her favorite Italian restaurant. She returned to the office a few minutes late but replete in body and restored in well-being.

The low hum of several voices came from David's office, and she checked her appointment book to see if she'd failed to write down a meeting. The space was blank so she decided, with a shrug, this was probably an impromptu thing that David had called during the lunch hour.

She tackled the filing pile from the morning's work and was busy at it when David's door opened. Before she could close the file drawer, a hand slid around the back of her neck and long fingers pressed against her jawline, turning her face around and up. Eyes wide with surprise, she saw Alek's blue eyes glitter with intent, and then his mouth claimed hers. In the few seconds her mouth was held captive she registered the expressions on the faces of the two men who had followed Alek out of David's office: David's face was a picture of uncertain concern, Terry Connors's of positive envy.

The two men stood watching as if frozen, then moved quickly toward opposite doors as Alek lifted his head. But not quickly enough to miss hearing Alek's words.

"I'm sorry about last night, darling, but the dinner lasted much later than I thought it would, and I didn't want to disturb you."

The doors facing them closed simultaneously. David's very gently, the other with a sharp snap.

Tara could have wept in pure frustration. Of course that sneaky Terry would have noticed the absence of Alek's car last night. That accounted for the speculative look he'd run over her this morning. And Alek? He was covering his tracks.

Seething with instant anger, she ignored the tingle in her fingers and lashed out, "You diabolical—!" She got no further, for Alek cut in with a silky warning.

"Careful, sweetheart. I told you before, no name-calling."

"Go to hell," she whispered angrily.

With a swift jerk he turned her fully around and she had to force herself to meet the blue flame of anger in his eyes.

"You're walking on very thin ice, my sweet. Take care you don't break through and find yourself in over your head." His voice was soft but chilling. "Why don't you give it up? Turn over your sword, hilt first, and we'll go on from there."

"I have no intention on going on to anything with you." For some reason Tara couldn't raise her voice above a whisper; she wet her lips, then went on. "So why don't you give it up? Leave me alone. Stop this madness."

"Madness? Hardly that." He laughed softly and planted a tiny kiss at the corner of her mouth. "Just a matter of chemistry. To be blunt, beautiful, you turn me on something fierce. I'd give you proof, but I don't think this is quite the time or the place."

Struck by the blatant audacity of the fiend, all she could find to say was, "Get out of here before I start screaming rape."

He laughed again, an easy, relaxed laugh that caused a vague sort of longing deep inside her; then, thank goodness, he walked to the door.

"Okay, kid, I'll let you get back to work. But I'm not nearly through with you yet."

After he'd gone, Tara turned back to the file cabinet, then paused with her hand on the drawer handle as an odd thought struck her. *Beautiful, sweetheart, kid.* The same words Terry had used on Monday morning. Alek had even thrown in *darling* and *my sweet.* Coming from Terry's mouth, the endearments had been offensive, an insult. Why then did they sound so exciting, somehow natural, from the lips of that hateful devil? The thought made Tara uncomfortable, and she pushed it away.

The remainder of the afternoon was a shambles. Try as she would, Tara could not seem to pull herself together, to still her trembling fingers. She made numerous typing errors, kept dropping things, and in the space of a few hours, almost wiped out her beautifully kept filing cabinets.

By the time she left the office, she was on the verge of tears. She ached, literally hurt all over, as if she'd been pulled through a hedge backward. While her teeth were punishing her lower lip as she walked to her car, her mind cried fiercely, *Why does he keep on with this?* Surely he knew by now how much she disliked, disapproved of him.

Sliding into the car, she slammed the door, jabbed the key into the ignition. She had thought, after that fiasco in his office on Monday . . . her hand paused on the key; hot pink color swept her cheeks. She could not, would not, let herself think about that.

Her fingers flipped the key, the engine fired into life, and with unthinking recklessness Tara drove off the lot and into the flow of traffic, ignoring the angry horn blasts from several irate drivers.

Where to go? What to do? she asked herself. She just couldn't face that apartment alone tonight. She was becoming positively claustrophobic in those small rooms. *Sallie?* Tara shook her head. *Explanations would have to be made. Who in the world would believe something like this?* Tara was having trouble believing it herself. Besides, Tara felt she had no right to endanger the working relationship between David and Alek.

Tara drove aimlessly for some time. Up one street, down another. Glancing around uninterestedly as she sat at a corner waiting for the light to change, Tara's eyes passed then came back to rest on a small tavern on the opposite corner. She had been in that tavern several times with friends. The food served was plain but good, the prices fair.

The light changed to green, and with sudden decision Tara hunted up a parking space, parked, and locked the car. A woman did not have to be afraid to enter this tavern alone. It was family owned and run. The wife did the cooking and serving, the husband tended the bar, and their son worked in both places, wherever he was most needed. They allowed, as they put it, no "funny business" in their place and they had posted a large sign to that effect. Both the owner and his son were big enough to back it up.

Though she rarely had a drink, Tara had suddenly decided she needed one. Hell! At this minute she felt she needed a dozen. Leaving the car, she skirted around the front entrance that led into the bar and entered the side door that opened into the dining room.

The room was half full of what Tara judged were neighborhood regulars. Moving toward the front of the building, Tara stopped at a small table, just inside the large open archway, that gave full view of the barroom. Young Jake Klinger, Jr., was working the end of the bar near the entrance to the dining room, and as Tara sat down he glanced up, grinned, and waved.

"Hi, Tara, howzit?"

Somehow she managed to return the grin convincingly.

"Fine, Jake, how are things with you?"

"Fair to middlin'," he replied laconically, then turned to serve his customer with the glass of beer he'd just tapped. That done, he sauntered around the end of the bar and to her table.

"What can I get you, gorgeous?"

Tara smiled, her eyes on the menu written in chalk on a blackboard hanging on the wall. After the lunch she'd eaten and the afternoon she'd put in, she didn't feel at all hungry. But she knew that if she drank and didn't eat, she'd be out for the count, or sick, in no time.

"I think I'll have a ham-and-cheese on dark rye and a Seven and Seven, please."

"You got it, baby."

Tara smiled again as Jake walked through the swing door into the kitchen, to give his mother the sandwich order. He was well named, truly a junior, for he looked remarkably like his father. Both Jakes were not very tall, but broad, built strong as bulls; they both had open, pleasant faces and gentle, compassionate brown eyes.

He paused on his way back, long enough to slide her sandwich plate in front of her, then went on into the bar to mix her drink. When Jake set the glass on the table, he said quietly, "This one's on me, sweet lips." Then he winked broadly, pursed his lips in a silent kiss, and went back behind the bar.

Tara laughed softly as she bit into her sandwich. Eating her sandwich without really tasting it, she pondered the different reactions male and female had to each other.

Jake's teasing familiarity amused her, whereas

80

Terry's use of endearments on Monday had made her feel cheap. As to the way she reacted to the same brand of teasing from Alek, well . . . she did not even care to think about that. Was it, as Alek had suggested, simple body chemistry?

By the time she pushed her empty plate to the center of the table, Tara was working on her third drink and telling herself to go home. Hearing a vaguely familiar voice say, "It's all right, I know the lady," Tara glanced into the barroom as a young man detached himself from the bar, a drink in each hand, and headed toward her.

As Tara watched him approach, her mind nibbled at recognition. Her memory clicked, and she put half a name to his face. Barry something-or-other, an architectural engineer she'd met last summer at a clambake she'd attended with friends. At the time, he'd appeared easygoing and well-mannered and Tara had agreed to go out with him the following week. It was a mistake for, although the evening had been a pleasant one, he had no sooner parked his car in front of her apartment when he was all over her like a bad rash. She had had literally to fight her way out of his car. And there was the reason she could not remember his last name. After she'd safely reached her apartment, she had dubbed him Barry Octopus. And now Mr. Octopus had come to stop at her table.

"Hiya, Tara, all alone?"

His grin was engaging (very probably practiced), revealing stunning white teeth (very probably capped). He had obviously taken to the style of permanents for men, for his previously straight, light-brown hair was now a mass of tiny curls on his well-shaped head. In tight, faded blue jeans and snug-

81

gly fitting knit shirt, he was very attractive and knew it.

"Yes, Barry, I'm alone."

Placing one of the drinks in front of her, he said quietly, "May I join you for a few minutes?"

Tara didn't want the drink. She didn't want his company either, but shrugging lightly, she murmured, "For a few minutes only. I'm leaving soon."

"Why? The night's young."

And you're so beautiful, Tara added, finishing his line wryly, somehow managing to keep a straight face.

"I've got a date later, that's why," she lied.

"Ah, yes, I've heard about your latest . . . date. Really moving up in the world, aren't you?"

Tara's voice was as cold as the glass her fingers clenched.

"If you're going to be offensive, Barry, you can go back to the bar, and take your drink with you."

He eyed her steadily a moment then he laughed easily.

"Truth hurt? Never mind. Hell, I wasn't trying to be offensive or then again maybe I was. After the cold shoulder I'd received, the pure-as-the-driven-snow act you'd put on, well, I'll admit when I first heard about it, I was shocked. He has a rather overwhelming reputation with women. But then he has a rather overwhelming bankroll also."

"Good-bye, Barry."

Tara was hanging on to her temper as tightly as she was hanging on to her glass.

Reaching across the table, his hand caught hers.

"Aw, come on, Tara," he coaxed. "With all the dames he's got on the string, surely he wouldn't object to you and I having a little fun together."

Eyes flashing with contempt, Tara snatched her hand away.

"Maybe *he* wouldn't, but I would," she said through clenched teeth. "Now go away and leave me alone."

Grasping for her hand again, he began urgently, "Don't get mad—"

"You having trouble, Miss Schmitt?"

With an audible sigh of relief, Tara looked up to see Jake senior leaning across the end of the bar, looking broad as a tank and just as menacing, eyeing Barry dispassionately.

"He was just leaving and so am I, Jake. Could I have my check please?"

"Sure thing," he nodded, then added, "Why don't you come back to the bar, Barry? I'll buy you a drink."

Barry hesitated then gave in gracefully.

"Okay, Jake, you're on. Sorry if I was out of line, Tara."

Ignoring Barry, Tara paid her check and left, feeling even worse than when she entered. The sight of Alek's car parked directly in front of her apartment plunged her spirits even lower.

Filled with rage, frustration, and humiliation, she paced the apartment for hours. First Terry, now Barry. How many others believed he was paying her rent, keeping her? Tears of weariness and defeat blinding her, she finally fell into bed. Teeth clenched, she whispered aloud, "Damn you, Aleksei Rykovsky."

Friday was a drag. Tara had never been so glad to see quitting time before in her life. As she left the office, she massaged her temple distractedly; she had a headache. Her eyes felt puffy and irritated from the hours she'd spent crying the night before. Lord, it seemed she'd had a headache and done nothing but cry for the last month. Was there no end to it?

Feeling too uninterested and dispirited to prepare a meal, she ate dinner at a small lunchroom close to her apartment then went home. Home? The lonely hours spent in solitude in those few small rooms were beginning to make what was once a haven into a cage. She felt trapped. Trapped by the unbridled passion of a man too used to getting what he wanted.

The tears were flowing again before she reached the door of her apartment, and the pain in her head had intensified into sharp, stabbing blows. Tara dropped her jacket and handbag on the nearest chair and went to the bathroom, groping blindly inside the medicine cabinet for the aspirin bottle. She swallowed the two white pills then stood regarding her reflection in the cabinet-door mirror. Watery, haunted eyes stared back at her, black-smudged mascara adding a clownish touch. What a pale, pitiful sight she was, she thought abstractedly. At nine thirty, head still pounding, she swallowed two more aspirin and went to bed, positive she wouldn't sleep.

She was wrong. She slept deeply and well and woke Saturday morning with at least some of her usual vigor restored. As she consumed a light breakfast of juice, toast, and coffee, her eyes roamed around the small kitchen. *What you need, friend,* she told herself bracingly, *is some physical activity. Today you clean the kitchen.*

Within minutes she'd thrown herself into the job at hand, saving the most hated chore, the kitchen stove, till last.

Tara had the rangetop in a half dozen assorted

pieces, scrubbing the drip pan under the burners, when the door chimes pealed.

"Oh, hell," she muttered, tugging the rubber gloves off her hands and dropping them in the sink. Walking to the door, she wondered if she should slide the chain into place, then shrugged and opened the door.

"May I come in, Tara? Or are you still mad at me?" Betsy eyed her uncertainly on the other side of the threshold.

"I'm not mad at you, Bets," Tara denied. "A little disappointed, maybe, but not mad. Come in."

Betsy stepped inside, slipped out of her long knit coat, and tossed it over a chair, all the while glancing around unobtrusively.

Tara watched her cynically, sighing softly with the knowledge her sister was looking for occupancy of a man.

"I'm cleaning the kitchen and was about ready to take a break," Tara said quietly. "Would you like a cup of coffee?"

"Yes, thanks," Betsy answered. "It's cold out there this morning. A hot drink will taste good."

Tara didn't miss the strained edge to her sister's voice, but she made no comment as she poured the coffee then placed the mugs, sugar bowl, and a small jug of milk on the table.

Betsy eyed her warily as she lit a cigarette then offered the pack to her, murmuring when Tara shook her head, "You quit?"

"I'm trying to," Tara answered. "I don't even have them around anymore." She hesitated, then said, "On second thought, I think I will have one, thank you." And added silently as she lit it, *I somehow think I'm going to need it.*

They sipped their coffee in an uncomfortable silence a few minutes, then Betsy blurted, "Tara, I think you should call Mama."

"Why? She hasn't bothered to call me." Tara was surprised at the bitterness of her own voice.

"I know," her sister said placatingly. "But I still think you should. I'm worried about her, Tara. You're the only one she ever opened up to at all. She won't talk to me. I've tried."

"Is she sick?" Tara asked in alarm.

"Not sick exactly," Betsy replied. "But she's not eating or sleeping well and she's been crying a lot."

Welcome to the club, Mama, Tara thought wearily, then forced her attention back to her sister as she continued.

"Do you think Mama could be going through the change of life?"

"I don't know. I suppose so, even though she is only forty-five. I've heard of women much younger going into it. And for that matter, much older, so I guess she could be." But for herself Tara was convinced her mother's trouble stemmed directly from the controversy surrounding her oldest child. "All right, Bets," Tara promised. "I'll call her later today and see if I can find out anything. Will you stay for lunch?"

"No. Thanks anyway. I've been skipping lunch." Then she added at Tara's raised eyebrows, "I've gained a few pounds and with the holidays coming up, I thought I'd better be careful or come January first, I'm liable to find I can't get into my clothes."

Tara smiled and relaxed at the more normal tone Betsy's voice had acquired. Not much later Betsy left, saying she had some shopping to do, and Tara went back to the stove.

After a hurried sandwich-and-coffee lunch, Tara went to the phone, drew a deep breath, and quickly dialed her mother's number. Her heart sank on hearing her father's gruff hello.

"Hello, Dad. Is Mother there?"

There was a noticeable pause before her father replied. "Yes, she's here. But she doesn't want to talk to you, Tara, and neither do I." And with that he slammed down the receiver.

Tara stood still, a look of hurt disbelief on her face, before slowly replacing her own receiver with trembling fingers. Feeling her eyes beginning to mist over, she shook her head in swift anger. No, she would not cry anymore; she was going to fight. *I don't know how I'll fight him,* she thought fiercely, *but I'll find a way. I have to. I can't take much more of this.*

To keep depression at bay she sprang into frenzied activity, giving the rest of the apartment its weekly cleaning, running to the basement laundry-room with a basket of wash, shampooing her hair, and manicuring her nails.

Sunday she walked for hours, coming back to the apartment cold and tired and nowhere near a way to get at Alek. A little after ten she sat moodily trying to concentrate, without much success, on a play on TV. Though Tara was unsure exactly what the play was about other than a philandering husband, one scene, near the end, caught then held her attention. The wronged wife was speaking to a friend in a harshly bitter tone. "He's offered me a large settlement if I'll give him a divorce." She laughed hollowly before continuing. "He should live so long, the sneaky rat. Oh! I'll get that money. That and a lot more. He'll pay through the nose. I'll make his life a living hell. By the time I'm through with him, he'll wish he'd never looked at a woman."

Tara sat nibbling her lip, a germ of an idea beginning to wriggle to life. Her breath caught painfully in her throat. Could she do it? Did she want to?

She set off to work Monday morning, her step firm and determined. No definite plan presented itself. She'd have to play it by ear, wing it, as it were. The morning passed slowly and although Tara became exceedingly more nervous, her resolve strengthened and set. All it needed now was the opportunity.

That arrived shortly after lunch when David came into the office, followed by a deceptively lazy-looking Alek. Before either man could speak, Tara said haltingly, "I—I'd like to speak to you, David. It's important."

David's voice mirrored the surprise on his face.

"All right, Tara." Then, turning to Alek, he murmured, "If you'll excuse us a few minutes."

Alek began, "Of course—" when Tara interrupted, "No! Please David, as this involves Alek too, I'd like him present."

Alek's eyes turned sharp, watchful, while David's expression changed from surprise to confusion.

"Whatever you say. Come into my office, both of you."

David waved his hand at the leather chair in front of his desk as he seated himself in his swivel chair opposite. Alek indicated he was quite comfortable where he was, perched indolently on the side of the large desk, which suited Tara, as she had an excellent view of both men's faces.

She let the silence hang a few seconds before stating quietly, "David, I want to give notice. I'm leaving."

"Give notice!" David exclaimed. "Leaving? But why?"

Tara's eyes sliced to Alek, then quickly away. In that brief glance she could swear he was holding his breath. She gulped in air, then said boldly, "I'm getting married and, even though we haven't discussed it, I don't think he wants me to work afterward." She swung her gaze directly to Alek's hooded blue one and added, "Do you—darling?" then held her breath.

He was a cool one, she had to give him that. For, other than a slight tightening along the jaw, he betrayed no reaction. One dark eyebrow arching slowly, he drawled, "While I would enjoy you giving your undivided attention to me, if you want to continue working, that is entirely up to you—my love." As he finished, the corner of his mouth twitched with amusement.

Tara gritted her teeth. *The fiend. I call his bluff and he has the gall to be amused.* She was beginning to wonder just who had called whose bluff.

David looked and sounded stunned. "Getting married? When?"

Tara hesitated only a moment. "The second Saturday in December."

"The second Saturday," he echoed, his eyes flying to his desk calendar. "But that's less than a month away. Why didn't you tell me sooner?" He turned to Alek, his voice sharp. "Or you? My God, man, we see each other nearly every day, and I've made no secret of how Sallie and I feel about Tara. Couldn't you have said something?"

Alek's smile was totally disarming. "I've been waiting, impatiently I might add, for the lady to set a date. This is as much of a surprise to me as it is to you." Glittering blue eyes were turned on Tara. "I didn't realize you had such a flair for the dramatic, my sweet."

"I think you'll find, my liege"—Tara's smile was pure saccharine—"I'm full of little surprises."

"I'll just bet." He laughed softly.

Throughout this exchange David's head swiveled from one to the other, a frown of consternation on his face. Catching the expression, Alek's laugh deepened. "Don't worry, David, you're not going to lose her, either as a friend or, apparently, as a secretary. That is, of course, if you're agreeable to her taking two weeks for a honeymoon, and the rest of the day."

Neither of the men seemed to notice Tara's gasp, as David was too busy shaking Alek's hand while acquiescing to his demands, and Alek was too busy grinning fatuously while accepting his congratulations.

Before Tara had time to gather her wits, Alek was grasping her arm and propelling her from both David's and her own office, pausing only long enough to snatch up her handbag and jacket. Flinging the latter around her shoulders, he led her out of the building and into his car.

"My car!" she squeaked.

"We'll get it later" came the brusque reply.

He drove without speaking for some time, leaving the city behind as he turned onto a country road nearly devoid of traffic. At the first roadside rest area, he pulled off the road and stopped. After turning off the ignition, he sat staring out the windshield, his silence somewhat ominous. When, after countless minutes, he finally spoke, she jumped, startled.

"You're committed now, you know. There will be no backing out." The hard edge to his tone softened somewhat as he asked, "Has something happened to effect this sudden change in your attitude?"

"It was brought home to me that I had very little choice," she replied softly, suddenly having to fight to keep tears from spilling over. "You have made a farce of all my hopes and plans. I'm afraid you're in for a shock if you're expecting an experienced woman. I'm one of the unmodern ones. I . . . I had thought to save my virginity for my husband, give it to him as a g-gift." Her last word was spoken on a strangled sob, and she turned her head away.

Tara heard his indrawn breath, felt him move a moment before his fingers, gently grasping her chin, turned her face back to him. His face was close, his voice very low. "And so you shall."

His mouth covered hers in a kiss both reticent and possessive; possession won. He drew her as closely to him as the console between the bucket seats would allow. Suddenly he released her and was moving away, cursing softly. Before she knew what he was about, he was out and around the car, yanking open the door next to her. In one unbroken movement he leaned inside, grasped her shoulders, pulled her out and into his arms. Shifting his weight to balance hers, he stood with his feet planted firmly a foot apart, crushing her body against the long, hard length of his.

He groaned softly and muttered, "God, Tara, I want you." Then his mouth began plundering hers hungrily, drawing from her a response she had had no idea she was capable of. His hands moved urgently over her body, arching her to him, giving her shocking proof of his words.

First the ground rocked, then the world spun, and she was drowning in a sea of intense, electrifying pleasure. Fire whipped through her veins, igniting pulse points and nerve ends in its wake. Arms tightening convulsively around his neck, teetering on the very edge of total surrender, she moaned a soft protest when his mouth left hers. Opening her eyes, she saw him glance around before murmuring huskily, "Where the hell can we go?"

His words brought a measure of unwanted sanity and with a choking sob she wrenched away from him to stumble sharply into the side of the car. She cried out in pain, but the pain brought further sanity, enabling her to plead, "No, Alek, stop," when he reached for her.

"No?" he rasped. "Stop? What are you trying to do, drive me mad?"

She was sobbing openly now, frightened badly, as much by her own body's astonishingly urgent need as his. Shaking her head, she sobbed wildly, "I'm frightened. You as much as promised me, not fifteen minutes ago, that you'd wait. I can't go on. Not here, not like this. Alek, please."

His face went hard, a muscle kicking in his taut jaw. His hands clenched into hard, white-knuckled fists, and he drew deep, long breaths. "All right, Tara." He groaned through clenched teeth. "We'll do it your way. But you can be grateful you set the day as closely as you did, for I'm damned if I'll wait one day longer."

His words chilled Tara, promising difficulties for her nebulous plans. It was not until later, on the way back to town, that she admitted ruefully to herself that he had gained control much more quickly than she. For while he was cool and withdrawn, handling the car with smooth expertise, she was still a humming bundle filled with awareness of him. And she knew that if he touched her now, she'd melt as quickly as a snowflake in August.

As they entered the city, Alek glanced at the expensive, slim gold watch on his wrist and said, "We have a few things to do before dinner. First I want to stop to make a phone call, and then we'll go shopping for your engagement ring."

His words jerked Tara away from her confusing emotions. "I don't want an engagement ring," she said flatly.

"Don't want . . . ?" he began, giving her a startled glance. Then his eyes hardened, grew icy. "Don't try playing games with me, Tara. You'll wear my ring." He finished grimly: "You said you'll marry me, and marry me you will."

"I'm not playing games," she replied coolly. "I have no intention of backing out of the marriage. But if you buy an engagement ring, I won't wear it. The only ring of yours I'll wear is my wedding ring."

His beautifully chiseled mouth flattened into a thin line.

"Why?"

"I simply do not want one."

Tara could feel his anger crackling outward, touching her, and she shivered.

He pulled up and parked at the first phone booth he came to, snapping, "I'll be back in a minute," and stepped out of the car, slamming the door behind him. He returned shortly, again slamming the door, turned, and gave her a smile that didn't quite make it to those glinting blue eyes.

"I phoned my mother. Told her I was bringing her future daughter-in-law to meet her and my father. We've been invited to dinner. I'm sure you'll want to bathe and change, as I do." His smile changed, becoming cruelly sardonic. "But first we'll stop at your parents' home. I'm sure your family, especially your father, will be delighted with our announcement."

Tara felt her blood turn to ice water and she shivered again. This was a ruthless man she was dealing with. Did she really have the courage to carry out her idea?

CHAPTER SIX

The closer they drew to her parents' home, the more tense and withdrawn Tara became. How would her parents react to Alek? Especially her father? He might fly into a rage. Hadn't he referred to Alek as "that Russian"? *"That swine Rykovsky"*? On the other hand he might be so relieved to know Alek was going to make an honest woman of her, he might accept his future son-in-law gracefully. *Too many* mights, she told herself nervously; *I might just be sick.*

Alek said nothing, but Tara caught the several eagle-eyed glances he threw at her. As they turned into the street her parents lived on, Tara noted the long fingers of golden afternoon sun. *Oh, great!* she thought. Not only would her father be home from work but by now Betsy would be too. One was never sure of her brothers, but this close to suppertime, they probably would be too. Her mother, of course, was nearly always home. Tara grimaced inside. A regular family conclave.

Alek parked at the curb in front of her parents' small frame home and said quietly, "Stay put," as her hand jerked to the door handle. Almost lazily, he left the car and moved around to open her door, helping her out as a lover would. Leaning close to her, he teased, "Someone may be watching from the window."

At any other time Tara would have walked, unannounced, into her father's house but now, after his crushing words to her on Saturday, she hesitated. Ignoring Alek's questioningly raised eyebrows, she placed a none-too-steady finger on the doorbell.

The door was opened a few inches by Karl, who gave her a disgusted look and complained, "What did ya ring the bell for, for cripes' sake?" He turned back into the hall at once, yelling, "Mom, Tara's here," not having seen Alek at all.

As she moved a few steps into the small hallway, Alek close behind her, she heard her father curse, then the rustle of a newspaper being flung to the floor.

Her father reached the doorway to the living room, George at his heels, just as her mother came hurrying along the short hall from the kitchen and Betsy came clattering down the stairs to stop abruptly in back of Karl, who had started up but had stopped and turned at their father's curse. All five began speaking at once.

"Tara, I told you on Saturday—"

"Oh, Tara, I'm so glad to see—"

"Tara, I thought you were going to call—"

"Gee, Tara, did you come in that car out—"

"Tara, what's going on any—"

"Be quiet, all of you."

The barrage ceased, Alek had not raised his voice, but the tone sliced through the babble like a rapier through butter. The tone of a man used to giving orders and having them obeyed without question: there were none.

The same tone broke the stunned silence as, eyes hard as the stone they matched, Alek addressed her father. "Mr. Schmitt, I'd like to speak to you in private a few minutes."

Eyes softening, he turned to her mother. "Perhaps you could give Tara a cup of coffee in the kitchen?"

"Yes, of course," her mother fluttered. "Come along, Tara. I just made a fresh pot for supper."

Tara hesitated, watching her father's angry red face, until he mumbled, grudgingly, to Alek. "All right, come into the living room." Then: "Make yourselves scarce, boys."

George threw a curious glance at Alek, then went up the stairs after Karl, and Tara followed her mother into the kitchen, Betsy right behind her.

Marlene poured coffee into two cups, placed them in front of Tara and Betsy, then asked, tremulously, "Who is that man, Tara? Why does he want to talk to your father alone?"

Before Tara could draw her attention from her mother's tired, unhappy face, Betsy answered excitedly, "That's none other than Mr. Aleksei Rykovsky, Mama." Turning wide eyes to Tara, she went on. "Why does he want to talk to Dad?"

Tara had been asking herself that same question. Surely it would have been easier to tell them all while they'd been gathered in the hall.

She contemplated what to answer as she sipped her coffee.

"Well, I'm not quite sure—"

"Marlene," her father's voice cut her off. "Come in here and bring Tara with you."

Biting her lip, her mother turned apprehensive eyes to Tara. Forcing a light laugh, Tara quipped, "I guess we'd better go and face the music." Swinging out of the kitchen, she answered, "May as well," to Betsy's "Can I come too?"

The two men stood facing each other across the room. Alek in front of the worn sofa, her father in front of his favorite chair. Tara took one step inside the room and stopped, her mother on one side, Betsy on the other. Apprehensively she glanced at Alek, then her father, then back to Alek again, unable to read anything in the face of either man.

"Come here, Tara."

Alek's voice was low, his tone gentle, and without question Tara went to him, her eyes trying to read his impassive face, the small smile playing at his mouth.

Her mother and Betsy followed her into the room and out of the corner of her eye she saw her brothers slip inside the doorway. Deliberately, it seemed to Tara, Alek had kept his eyes on her face until they were all in the room, then he turned that brilliant blue gaze on her mother and said quietly, "Mrs. Schmitt, your husband has just given me his permission to marry your daughter. I sincerely hope you will give yours also."

He had asked for permission! Alek Rykovsky! Incredible, Tara thought. Tara felt her breath catch, heard Betsy's small "oh," saw her mother go pink, glance at her husband then back at Alek before stuttering, "I-I—if Herman says—"

"He does," Herman interrupted. Then, as if suddenly becoming aware that they were all standing, he said, "Won't you sit down, sir?"

Too much! Tara thought. She stared at her father. The only other men she'd ever heard her father speak to in that deferential manner were their priest and doctor. And not always their doctor.

Alek murmured "Thank you," lowered himself to the sofa then held his hand out, palm up, and said softly, "Tara."

Bemused, Tara sat down next to him, placed her hand in his large, well shaped one, and felt it squeezed as he said to her mother, "Tara and I would like to be married on the second Saturday in December. I hope there will be enough time to make the necessary arrangements."

Her mother's eyes flew to her, and Tara answered hurriedly, "Yes, of course there'll be enough time. A small wedding really doesn't take much arrange—"

"You'll naturally want to be married in your own church," he cut in smoothly. "But I hope you'll have no objections to my own priest presiding."

Tara turned astonished eyes to him. "You're Catholic, Alek?"

"Yes, my love, I am." Again that small smile played around his mouth. She watched it in fascination, then his actual words struck her.

"In church?" she choked. "But that's not necessary. I thought a quiet wedding, no fuss."

She heard her father snort, her mother exclaim, "But Tara!" But Alek again commanded the floor.

"We will have a full Catholic wedding, darling. Including mass. We're only going to do this once; we may as well do it right. You may have as few or as many attendants as you wish." The devil danced in his eyes as he added, "Just don't exhaust yourself with the preparations."

Tara felt her cheeks flush at his meaning: He didn't want an overtired bride on his wedding night.

She felt his arm slide around her waist, draw her closer to him. *What's he playing at now*, she wondered fretfully. Then was surprised at the explanation that leaped into her mind. The endearments, the touching, the tone of voice were all calculated to assure her father, all of them, that she was loved, cared for, protected. *But why would he bother to do that?* she argued with herself. *He had what he wanted. At least he* thought *he did.* Nevertheless the feeling persisted that he was deliberately acting the role of a man very much in love simply to reassure her parents.

The action of Alek glancing at his watch forced Tara's attention back to the conversation. He was speaking to her father, and his words jolted her alert.

"And, as I just said, the number of the wedding party, the type of wedding, is entirely up to Tara, but if you have no objections, I will arrange the reception." He held up one hand as both her father and mother started to protest. "Let me finish, please. I'm afraid it will be, by necessity, both rather large and expensive. I have quite a few friends and business associates. I would not want to have any one of them feel slighted because they were not invited. Many of them will be coming from a distance. Not only from out of town, but out of state as well. Arrangements must be made for their accommodations." Until this point his voice had been smooth, almost soft. Now it took on a thin, hard edge. "I insist on paying for it, as the majority of the names on the guest list will come from me." He glanced at her mother, and again the tone grew gentle. "I would appreciate it if you could have your guest list completed within a few days. We have less than a month, and I'd like the invitations in the mail by the end of this week."

"The end of this week!"

"But Alek, that's impossible."

Tara and her mother spoke in unison. Tara was too surprised to say anymore, but her mother continued. "That's not nearly enough time. Not only do we have to make up the guest list but we have to see the printers, pick out the invitations—"

"That won't be necessary," he interrupted. "Just make up your list as quickly as possible. My staff will take care of the rest. The invitations will be handwritten. Believe me, you will be satisfied with the result."

"Well, if you say so," her mother murmured.

Tara was beginning to feel very uneasy. When had she lost control of this farce? She was actually not being consulted at all, for all his talk of the size of the wedding being up to her. Feeling that she had to make some sort of stand she said, firmly, "Alek, I really do not want a large wedding. I had thought a small, quiet affair with just the families and maybe a few close friends."

The wicked gleam in his eyes alerted her, yet his words shocked her, causing a momentary hush in the room. "My sweet love, would you deprive the rest of our friends, everyone, the pleasure of witnessing the culmination of the union about which there has been so much speculation?"

Tara felt tears sting her eyes. "Alek." It was a low cry of protest, almost instantly covered by the hurried speech of nearly everyone in the room.

"It is settled." Alek's tone indicated he would listen to no arguments.

"Well then, Tara," Marlene said briskly. "You and I had better get working on a list."

"Not this evening," Alek stated. "Tara and I have a dinner engagement with my parents." He paused a moment then went on. "Darling, as it appears you are going to have to be spending a lot of time here anyway, why don't you pack what you'll need and move in here until the wedding. We can empty your apartment at our leisure later."

Tara stared at him in stunned amazement, unable, for a minute, to speak. *Too fast*, she told herself. *Everything was happening much too fast*. Why had she told David the second Saturday in December? She was beginning to feel rushed, stifled. And who did he think he was? *We? Our?* And she definitely did not want to move back here. She opened her mouth to say no, but not fast enough.

"Tara, that's a wonderful idea." Her mother's eyes were bright with excitement and enthusiasm. "It would save you all that running back and forth. Oh, honey, please, it will be such fun."

The word *no* trembling on her soft mouth, Tara sighed in defeat, unable to utter the word that would extinguish the light in her mother's eyes, cast a shadow on the happy face. But Alek would hear more about this later.

"All right, Mama," Tara answered tiredly. "I'll bring my things one night this week."

"I'll bring her and her things," Alek inserted. "Tomorrow night. If that's convenient." He didn't look at Tara's angrily flushed face, but kept his polite gaze on her mother, acknowledging her nod with a smile.

"I have my own car," Tara said through gritted teeth.

"Yes, darling, I know that." His words came slowly, evenly measured, as if he were speaking to a child who was not too bright. "Nevertheless, I will bring you tomorrow night. Now I think we really must go, as Mother is expecting us in an hour and a half."

His hand firmly grasping hers, he stood up and strode across the room, hand outstretched to her father. "A pleasure to meet you, sir. I assume we'll be seeing quite a bit of each other during the next few weeks?"

"Yes, yes, of course," Herman hastened to assure him, "and a pleasure to finally meet you, Mr. Rykovsky."

"Alek. I insist." His tone was so silky-smooth, Tara felt her teeth clench. He wished her mother a gentle good night, then started to move out of the room. He paused to raise an eyebrow at Betsy and murmur, "I'm depending on you to help Tara with all the arrangements. Will you do that?"

"Are you kidding?" Betsy laughed. "I'd like to see someone stop me."

He grinned, then moved on only to stop again at George.

"You're in your last year of high school?" he asked abruptly.

George nodded, eyes guarded.

"You're going to college?"

"If I can get a scholarship. Why?"

Alek studied him a second, then, as if reaching a swift decision, gave a brief nod and said, "If you want a job after school, come to see me. And if the scholarship doesn't materialize, we'll have a talk. Good night." He turned his head to include Karl, then made for the hall and their coats, tugging Tara behind him.

He held her coat for her, then shrugged into his

own, bid them all a collective good night and, his hand at her back, propelled her out of the house. By the time he had seated her in the car, the dazed, steamrollered feeling had passed and Tara was doing a slow burn.

"How dare you," she seethed the instant he slid behind the wheel.

"How dare I what?"

Her hands clenched at his innocent tone. "Damn you, you know what," she snapped. "I do not want a large wedding and I certainly do not want to move back home and I damn well will not have you arranging my life."

"Don't swear at me again, Tara." His voice, while soft, had a warning edge of steel in it.

"All right," she sighed, "I'm sorry. But I mean it, Alek. Don't think for one minute that just because I agreed to marry you, I have any intention of playing the meek little hausfrau, blindly obeying your every dictate. I won't."

"Whatever you say, sweetheart. Now please stop nagging at me as if we were already married and look at that lovely moon. Not quite full but beautiful anyway."

The sound of his soft laughter seemed to wrap itself around her heart, and Tara had to remind herself sharply who he was and what he'd done.

"I don't want to look at the moon," she said irritably. "And I don't really want to have dinner with your parents, although I suppose we owe them a courtesy visit. And don't call me 'sweetheart.' Save your breath, and the endearments, for your next audience."

She heard his sharply indrawn breath, saw his

hands tighten on the steering wheel before he growled, "I will call you anything I wish, when I wish. I'm sorry if the prospect of meeting my parents is repellent to you, but you may be in for a surprise. I'd be willing to bet you'll like them. They are very nice people."

In this he was proved correct. They *were* very nice people, and she did like them. He had dropped her at the apartment with a terse, "I'll be back in a half hour. Can you be ready by then?" At her nod he said, "Good," sharply. The moment she was out of the car, he shot away from the curb, still obviously very angry.

The drive to his parents' home was completed in tense silence, which Tara herself broke unconsciously when he drove along the driveway and parked in front of the sprawling redwood-and-glass ranch house.

"Oh, it's beautiful!" she breathed softly. Tara had expected something large and formal and this lovely rambling house was a delightful surprise.

"Yes, it is," Alek replied softly. "And so are the people who live in it."

Tara had known she'd angered him with her waspish words about not wanting to meet his parents, but now something about the tone of his voice told her he had also been hurt. *Impossible,* she said to herself, pushing the thought away. Nothing she could say to this unfeeling man could hurt him.

On entering, Tara was delighted to find the inside as lovely as the outside. It was decorated beautifully in soft, muted tones, the overall effect one of warmth, welcome. The warmth and welcome were reflected on the face of the woman who came to meet them, hands outstretched.

"Darling, you're right on time." The low, musical voice of Alek's mother's was not a surprise, coming from such an exquisitely beautiful woman. Small, splendidly proportioned, she had the most perfect bone structure Tara had ever seen. *So this is where he came by his devastating good looks,* she thought.

Before Alek could murmur more than, "Good evening, Mother," she was speaking again, taking Tara's hands in her own. "And this is Tara. Such a lovely name, and what a lovely thing you are too. No wonder Alek is in such a rush to get you to the altar. But come in, please, we have just enough time for a drink before dinner. And here's Peter, right on time to mix them."

Tara was forced to change her opinion of a few moments ago. For coming toward her was the original mold from which Alek had been made. One glance and Tara knew exactly what Alek would look like in twenty-five years. After the introductions were made, Peter Rykovsky tilted one dark brow at his son and said quite seriously, "Well, son, I didn't think it possible, but you have found yourself a woman whose beauty matches your mother's. My deep and sincere congratulations."

"Thank you, sir."

Pink-cheeked, Tara glanced at Alek in astonishment for the tone of respect he'd conveyed in those three short words.

As they sipped their drinks, Alek filled his parents in on the wedding plans they had made earlier. Peter and Alene's reaction to Tara's idea of a small, intimate wedding was the same as her own family's had been.

"Oh, no, my dear," Alene reproved gently. "I'm

sure that would be a mistake. Every girl should be able to remember her wedding day as being as perfect as possible. By all means keep the wedding party small, if that's what you prefer. A wedding doesn't have to be large to be beautiful. But I do think Alek is right in his insistence on a church ceremony." Her soft laughter gave proof of the happiness bubbling inside as she added, "I must admit to a degree of selfishness in my considerations. I have waited so long for this day. When Alek celebrated his thirty-fourth birthday last spring, I decided, perhaps I had better resign myself to the idea of his remaining a bachelor and never giving me the grandchild I so long to hold."

Tara started, paling visibly, although her reaction went unnoticed. Alek and his father wore identical expressions of deep love and tenderness as they gazed on the misty-eyed, wistful, but adoring face of Alene. Tara felt terrible. Motivated by anger and frustration, she had acted without thought, now the ramifications of that act were piling up around her like so many stones, imprisoning her inside a cell of her own making. Panic gripped her throat, and she gulped the remains of drink in an effort to dislodge it.

A grandchild! Not once had she considered that possibility. Why hadn't she? It was the natural order of things. First the wedding, then . . . A shiver rippled through her body. Her own parents had not said anything but they, too, would be looking forward to their first grandchild—after a decent interval. *Oh, Lord!* Tara's mind clung to her last thought. *A decent interval!* Everyone thought she and Alek were already lovers. Now suddenly they were being married within a few weeks. How many of her friends would be counting the months? Watching for signs? *But I've done nothing, nothing,* her mind cried silently, envisioning the different type of speculative glances she would probably now be receiving. A feeling of intense dislike—almost hatred—for Alek burned through her and she closed her eyes.   . .

Locked in a pain-filled world of her own, Tara was startled by Peter's voice, heavily laced with concern, alerting her to where she was.

"Tara, child, are you ill? You've gone positively white."

She saw Alek's gaze swivel from his mother's face to her own an instant before he was moving to her side. His eyes, his face, puzzled her, for he looked almost frightened. Alek frightened? His softly murmured words chased all contemplation of his expression from her mind.

"What's wrong, darling. Are you ill?"

The endearment set her teeth on edge and she had to fight to keep from screaming at him, *You fraud, you are what is wrong. You and the scheming and plotting you've done.* Using every ounce of willpower she possessed, she brought her emotions under control. "I'm afraid the drink has hit rock bottom," she lied shakily. "I've eaten very little all day, and my empty stomach doesn't seem to want to tolerate the alcohol."

Long, unbelievably gentle fingers brushed her cheek, felt the moisture that had gathered at her temple.

"Would you like to go home?"

Jerkily she leaned back, away from his caressing voice, his disturbingly light touch. *Yes,* she pleaded silently, *I want to go home. I want to hide myself*

108

away until everything that has happened the last week is long forgotten.

"Would you like to lie down, my dear?" Peter asked anxiously.

Before Tara's confused mind could formulate an answer to either man, Alene was helping her to her feet, stating practically, "What this child needs is some food. Come along, Tara," she coaxed. "Something solid inside your stomach will banish this queasy feeling in no time." Leading Tara into the dining room, she shook her head in mock dismay, chiding, "Men are so helpless in situations like this. For some reason the strongest of them, and these two must be close to the top of the list, fall apart when someone they love is unwell."

A bubble of hysterical laughter became trapped in Tara's chest. If Alek was close to the top of the list of the strongest, he had to be even higher on the list of best actors if he could convince his mother with his performance.

Alene's diagnosis proved correct, for by the time they were halfway through the meal, Tara, her color restored, was laughing at Peter's obvious attempts to amuse her.

Tara was totally captivated by Alek's parents and under any other circumstances would have loved having them as in-laws. Strange, she mused, Peter and Alek were so much alike, yet she failed to detect any sign of the tyrant in Peter. His treatment of his wife was the type great love stories were written about; after nearly forty years of marriage his eyes touched her with an expression that Tara could only describe as adoration. Tara quickly learned where Alek had acquired the art of using endearments with such ease of manner. Peter seldom spoke to Alene without some form of endearment. That his feelings were returned in full was evident: Alene made no attempt to hide the fact that her world revolved around her husband and son.

As Tara basked in the warmth Alene and Peter generated, the evening slipped away from her. The only thing that marred her enjoyment was the caressing, possessive tone Alek used whenever he spoke to her.

When he drove her home, he pulled up in front of her building and said, "It's late, I won't come up with you." Tara breathed a sigh of relief then tensed as his hands cupped her face and drew her close. He kissed her slowly, lingeringly, and Tara felt the tenseness seep out of her, tiny little sparks igniting all over her.

When he lifted his head, he again whispered those same Russian words then said, "As your car is still on the office parking lot, I'll drive you to work tomorrow. Is seven thirty all right?"

"Y-Yes, that will be fine," Tara stammered. "I—I must go in. Good night."

There was no conversation exchanged between them the next morning other than a polite "Good morning, Tara," and an equally polite "Good morning, Alek," until he drew up at the office. Placing a hand on her arm as she moved to get out of the car, he said, "I'll come by at seven thirty to help you with your things."

Impotent anger surged through Tara and, pulling her arm away from his hand, she snapped, "All right," then thrust open the door and slammed it shut, his laughter following her as she hurried into the building.

"Tara, you really know how to keep a secret. Why didn't you tell us?" Jeannie's words hit her as she came through the door, but she was saved from confusion by the newspaper Jeannie shoved in front of her. In a lower corner of the front page was a picture of Alek with the caption LOCAL INDUSTRIALIST TO WED. Tara skimmed the small column that ran the length of the picture then pasted a smile on her face as she looked up at Jeannie. "If I'd told you, it wouldn't have been a secret. Besides, we wanted to discuss it with our parents first."

When had he done this, she thought furiously. Somehow she managed to maintain the smile as she glanced around the room murmuring thank-yous to the good wishes being called out. Her eyes brushed Terry then came back. The only words to describe the expression on his face were utter disbelief. His eyes seemed to ask, How did you do it when all the others failed?

With a forced note of happiness she asked Jeannie if she could borrow the paper then, still smiling, she went into her own office, dropped into her chair, and read the article more thoroughly.

Mr. Aleksei Rykovsky, son of Mr. and Mrs. Peter Rykovsky, owner-manager of the Fine Edge Machine Company, has announced his forthcoming marriage to Miss Tara Schmitt, daughter of Mr. and Mrs. Herman Schmitt. A December wedding is being planned. Miss Schmitt is the confidential secretary of Mr. David Jennings, one of the city's up-and-coming architects and the designer of the new plant Mr. Rykovsky is having built.

David came in the office, paper under his arm, as Tara was finishing the article. "I brought you the paper, but I see you already have one."

"Yes," she replied sweetly, lifting the sheet. "Plugs for everyone. Isn't that nice?"

David gave her an odd look then shrugged and headed for his office. "Oh, yes. I almost forgot. Sallie asked me to give you her very best wishes."

Sallie! Oh, Lord, Tara groaned inwardly, *I should have called her. But when?* She reached for the phone and dialed David's home number. Sallie answered on the third ring.

"Hi, Sallie. It's Tara."

"Tara! Oh, I'm so glad you called. Did David give you my message?"

"Yes, thank you." Somehow she managed to instill the lilt of happiness into her voice. "Sallie, I know it's short notice, and we'll be rushed like mad, but please say you'll be my matron of honor."

Sallie's light laughter danced along the wire. "Of course I will, I'd have been crushed if you hadn't asked me. When can we get together?"

"Could you get away for a few hours tomorrow night? Come over to my mother's?"

"Yes, certainly. Your mother's?"

Tara knew she'd have to make an explanation that was convincing. Sallie knew all too well how she felt about living at home.

"Yes, I'm going to move back home until the wedding. With so much to do in so little time, I'm hoping to save wear and tear on my nervous system."

"Probably the best idea," Sallie replied, musingly. Tara exhaled very slowly with relief as Sallie added, "I'll come over right after dinner, okay?"

"Fine, I'll see you then. Now I'd better get to work before the boss catches me goofing off. Bye, Sal."

Tara hung up, Sallie's happy laughter ringing in her ears. She felt a growing sense of panic, as if she were caught in a net and someone was drawing it tighter and tighter. What had she started?

CHAPTER SEVEN

That evening Tara stood in her bedroom, suitcases open on the bed, clothes scattered around them, when the doorbell rang at exactly seven thirty.

"Oh, rats," she muttered under her breath then stormed out of the bedroom to the door. Turning the lock, she flipped the door open, spun on her heel, and stalked back into the bedroom without even glancing into the hall.

Staring in disgust at the cases and clothes a few minutes later, Alek's voice, low, menacing, touched her like a cold breeze. "Don't ever do that again, Tara."

Surprise turned to shock when she swung her head to stare at him. He was standing just inside the bedroom doorway, and his stance, everything about the hard look of him, was more chilling, menacing than his voice had been.

"Do what?" Tara wet her dry lips, suddenly frightened. "What did I do?"

His tone was harsh, the words clipped. "Don't ever unlock your door and turn away without looking to see who it is again. Are you looking to get robbed, or mugged, or worse?"

"But I knew it was you." Tara made her voice hard in an effort to hide the fear curling in her chest.

"You thought it was me," he rapped. "Not quite the same thing."

Unable to face that brittle blue stare, she turned her head to gaze unseeingly at the bed. Shock was added to shock at his lightning change of mood. His tone was now light and teasing, he sauntered across the room to her, eyes flicking over the cluttered bed.

"I thought you'd be almost finished packing by this time."

Anger replaced the fear inside and, without pausing to think, Tara flashed, "I don't know what to take and what to leave. I don't want to go to my mother's. I want to stay here in my own place. I'm used to my freedom. Do you realize that not only will I lose my privacy, I'll have to share a bedroom with Betsy?"

"Get you used to the idea of sharing a room," he teased laughingly.

In exasperation she turned glaring eyes to him. "Damn you, Alek, it's not funny."

Before the last word was out, she knew she'd gone too far. His face went hard, and his hands shot up to grip her upper arms, his long fingers digging in painfully. "I told you not to swear at me again," he growled dangerously.

She opened her mouth to apologize but not quickly enough. He pulled her against his hard chest, and his mouth crushed hers punishingly, brutally. Her hands, flat against his chest, pushed futilely at him, and she tried vainly to pull away from him. His one hand released her and, with a low, swinging arc, his arm swept the cases from the bed. His hand regripped her arm and he turned her, pushing her back and down. Her back hit the bed, his full weight on top of her, and she felt her breath explode inside her chest. The fear she had experienced earlier was nothing compared to the blind panic that now clutched at her throat.

Like a wild thing she struggled against him, hands pushing, legs kicking. Twisting her head frantically, she finally succeeded in tearing her mouth away from his cruel, bruising lips. Gasping for air, she choked, "You're nothing but an unprincipled savage. You're hurting me."

His darkened eyes glittered into hers, and he rasped, "Sometimes I'd like to do more than hurt you. At times I'd like to break your stiff neck." His mouth sought hers again, and Tara jerked her head away, feeling his lips slide roughly across her cheek. He was still a moment, then his hand moved from her arm, sliding slowly to the beginning swell of her breast. Lips close to her ear, he groaned, "Tara, in a few weeks I'll be your husband. Surely a few weeks can't make all that much difference." His hand slid caressingly over her breast and, his voice a harsh whisper, he urged, "Tara, let me. Let me."

Tara had to fight a different kind of fear now. The fear of the betraying, yielding softness invading her body.

"No," she cried. "Alek, you promised me."

His cool breath caressed her cheek as he sighed, then lifted his hand and pushed himself up and away from her. He stood tense, staring at her broodingly for a long minute before snapping, "All right, let's gather this stuff together and get the hell out of here before I change my mind." The thought flashed into

116

Tara's mind that this was the reason for his insistence she stay with her parents. Was he afraid that the inevitable would happen if they were alone here? She shook her head in negation. *No, not Alek. Too out of character*. His reason was obvious. While she was surrounded by her family, there was less chance she'd change her mind, call the whole thing off.

By nine o'clock Tara was settled into her sister's room. Betsy had emptied some drawers and made room in the closet for her things, then stayed to help her unpack.

After the scene in her apartment bedroom, they had made fast work of the packing. Alek had carried the heavier things down the stairs and stowed them in his trunk. Then he had followed her car in his own to her father's house, where her brothers had taken over, lugging the cases up to Betsy's room.

Tara and Betsy were stowing the cases under the twin beds when their mother called, "I've made coffee, girls. Come have a cup while it's hot."

The sisters grinned at each other at the term *girls* then, side by side, went down the stairs and into the living room to join Alek and their parents.

"Well, Tara, come sit down. You look so tired, you're pale." Her father's changed attitude toward her was a secret source of amusement to Tara, and she had to work at controlling the twitch on her lips—a job made almost impossible when she encountered the wickedly laughing gleam in Alek's eyes.

"Yes, darling, come sit next to me and have some coffee. It will help you relax."

Although she did as he asked, Tara was convinced that if she was to relax, the last place in the world for her to sit was next to Alek.

117

As they drank their coffee, they discussed their plans for the next few days. Tara told her mother about having Sallie for her matron of honor, and that Sallie would be coming over tomorrow night. Then, glancing at her hopeful-faced sister, she grinned and said teasingly, "I hope you'll agree to be my maid of honor, as I'm planning on it."

"Oh, Tara." Betsy laughed shakily. "I was beginning to be afraid you weren't going to ask me."

"Not ask you? You nit, do you think I'd get married without you?"

Tara's voice was a little shaky, and she was glad when her mother turned the conversation to Alek.

"Have you decided on a best man yet, Alek?"

"Yes, I have. As a matter of fact I spoke to him today. My cousin Theo assured me he'd be delighted to prop me up, so to speak."

"Your cousin lives here in Allentown?" her father asked.

"No, Theo lives in Athens." At her parents' startled expression he explained briefly: "My mother's sister married a Greek. The Zenopopoulos family is a very old, respected one. Their firstborn son, Theo, runs the family shipping line now that my uncle Dimitri has retired."

"You have something of an international family, it appears," Tara said quietly.

His eyes came back to hers; his smile was pure charm.

"Yes, my sweet, I suppose I have. But only on my mother's side. She was born in Great Britain and her mother, now widowed, still lives in London, as does her brother, my uncle Edward. Her eldest brother, William, married a girl from Scotland. They live in

Edinburgh. My father is second-generation American. He and I are the only ones left, as his parents are both dead, and he was an only child. As I am."

"I see," Tara replied, not quite sure she understood the underlying inflection he'd placed on his last words.

"Do you, my love? I wonder."

Confused, feeling as if she'd missed an important point, Tara changed the subject. "I think we'd better work on the guest list tonight," she said to her mother. "Have you had a chance to work on it at all today?"

"I've finished it." Marlene slanted a quick glance at her husband before adding, "Your father and I worked on it last night after you left."

Will wonders never cease? Tara asked herself wryly, somehow managing to keep the surprise she felt from showing. Her father's complete change of face since Alek had spoken to him the night before was both a source of amusement and irritation. It was as if he felt that now he had to handle her with kid gloves so as not to damage the merchandise Alek had claimed as his own. Tara couldn't decide if she wanted to laugh out loud or scream at him. What she had suspected weeks ago had been proved correct. Her father, recognizing in Alek the top dog of arrogant tyrants, had capitulated completely. Mentally tossing her head at the funny little games men played, Tara offered, "I'll go over the list later and add my own to it. It will be ready tomorrow, Alek."

He left soon after that, drawing her with him when he stepped out the door. Her hand firmly on the doorknob to prevent the door from closing entirely, she shook her head when he asked, "I won't be seeing you at all tomorrow night?" His eyebrows went up in question when she replied, "Or Thursday." At his expression she added hurriedly, "I want to go shopping. The gowns must be selected as soon as possible."

He frowned but murmured, "All right, but don't make any plans for Friday. We're having dinner together. I'll come for you at seven."

She had no time to answer, for, bending his head, his lips caught hers in a light kiss that proceeded swiftly to one that was hard and demanding. She stood passive, her lips cool under his, for a few seconds. Then, frightened by the warmth spreading through her body, she pushed her arm against the door and stepped back into the comparative safety of the brightly lit hallway. His eyes flashed with irritation, and she whispered breathlessly, "I must go in, Alek, I'm cold."

"I could have warmed you," he murmured harshly as he turned abruptly and walked to his car.

I no longer doubt it, Tara admitted to herself somewhat fearfully.

Sallie stopped by, as planned, the following evening and after a few hours of haggling with everyone in the house, Tara had her own way. They all protested, but Tara was determined to keep the wedding party small. Betsy and Sallie would be her only attendants.

Right after dinner Thursday evening, Tara, her mother, Betsy, and Sallie set out for the most exclusive bridal shop in town. Tara had no preconceived idea of what she wanted but she chose the second gown she looked at, paling slightly when the salesclerk told her the price. The other three women took much longer in selecting their gowns, enjoying themselves immensely, trying on gown after gown, while Tara sat, shifting restlessly in her chair, smoking one cigarette after another. Glancing at the growing number of cigarette butts, she grimaced in self-disgust. *I'm hooked again,* she thought sourly. *Another thing I have to thank Alek Rykovsky for.*

She and Alek did not go out for dinner on Friday evening after all. As Sallie was preparing to go home after they'd returned from shopping, having gone from the bridal shop to a shoe store, she said gayly, "Tara, David and I have planned an engagement party for tomorrow night. Just a small gathering, casual dress, so I'll see you then."

Tara felt suddenly panicky at the prospect of facing the rest of her friends for the first time since the wedding announcement and she stammered, "But, Sallie, I—I don't know, I mean, I don't think Alek—"

"Don't be silly," Sallie interrupted. "David spoke to Alek about it this afternoon and he said Alek was delighted. Now I've got to run. See you tomorrow night. Bye."

The party was an ordeal for Tara. She dressed casually but carefully in a peacock-blue evening pantsuit in crepe de chine, which moved and flowed with and around her body as she walked. After a light application of makeup, she stepped back from the mirror to observe the overall effect and smiled with satisfaction. Alek's expression, as he ran his eyes slowly over her, was an added boost to her confidence. But it was short-lived, slipping away to be replaced by growing nervousness and tension, as she fought to maintain the picture of the happy bride in front of her friends.

The evening seemed to drag on forever, Alek's possessive attitude and endearments making her alternatively angry and more nervous. When it was finally over and they were back in Alek's car on their way home, she let her head fall back against the seat and sighed with exhaustion. There would be more parties of this type, and she knew it and prayed for the strength to get through them with at least some degree of aplomb.

Her mind was drifting aimlessly when he brought the car to a stop in front of her parents' house, and her body jerked in alarm when his hands cupped her face, and he touched her mouth with his own. Turning her face, sliding her mouth from his, she whispered, "Alek, please, I'm so tired. All I want to do is go to bed."

Her action had placed her ear close to his lips and he replied, urgently, "Not nearly as badly as I do."

The words, his tone, sent a shaft of such intense longing through Tara, she was shocked, suddenly frightened. She didn't understand these feelings he could so easily arouse, and in sheer self-defense, she whipped up her anger. Her hand gripped the door handle and pushed the door open as she moved away from him. "I'm going in," she snapped. Then she turned to look directly at him and observe, "It seems to me that the only things men think about are sex and money."

"And that's bad?" He laughed softly.

"Don't laugh at me, Alek," she warned.

"All right, I won't," came the indulgent reply.

"And don't patronize me either," she cried, turning to jump from the car.

His hand grasped her arm, forced her around to

122

face him. "Whoa, take it easy." His eyes glittered, his voice held a touch of concern. "You *are* tired. You sound like you're ready to fly into fourteen different directions at once. Sleep in tomorrow. I told you, I didn't want you wearing yourself out."

His last statement brought color to her pale cheeks, a flash to her tired eyes. Who the hell was he to tell her anything?

"Let me go, Alek." She spoke through gritted teeth to keep from screaming at him. "I'm going inside."

Slamming the door as she got out of the car, Tara ran up the walk and had the key in the door lock when Alek caught up with her. His arms slid around her waist, pulling her back against him, crushing the velvet of the long evening cape she'd thrown over her shoulders.

"Tara, I know this evening wasn't easy for you, but don't you think you're overreacting a little?" His breath was a soft caress against her hair, and in a weak moment Tara let her head rest on his hard chest. "If you allow yourself to get this uptight every time we're in the company of our friends, you'll be a total wreck in no time. Relax. Enjoy the attention you're receiving as the bride-to-be. The decision to marry was yours, you know."

Renewed anger banished weariness temporarily and, twisting away from his arm violently, she said bitterly, "Oh, yes, I know, the final decision was mine. But I was left with little choice and I didn't want, nor can I enjoy, the attention of my friends." Sarcasm overlaid the bitterness as she added, "Now, if I have your permission, I'd like to go in."

"Tara!"

"Good night, Alek."

With that she turned the key, pushed the door open, stepped inside, and shut the door firmly on his face.

The following two weeks rushed by hectically, Tara constantly fighting down the growing feeling of panic. What had she started? Would she go through with it? Was there any way she could stop it now? She knew the answer to that. Her mother's happy face, as she sat carefully numbering the increasing flow of wedding gifts and arranging them on a long folding table her father had set up in the living room, gave it to her. There was a sparkle in her eyes as she smoothed work-reddened hands over the white tablecloth and touched, again and again, the obviously expensive gifts. She looked years younger and laughed often, and Tara felt trapped, afraid to go ahead, unable to step back. Betsy and Sallie were enjoying the preparations almost as much as her mother and through it all Tara plastered a smile on her face.

She could find no escape, even in the office, and the smile grew brittle. Suddenly all the friends who'd been silent for weeks became very vocal and Tara had to fight down a mushrooming cynicism. God! She had never been so popular in her life. Totally unimpressed, she moved through the days, giving all the proper answers, laughing at all the proper times, and withdrew into her own hiding place inside herself. Denied even the solace of a room of her own, she cried inside, bitter, resentful tears that never touched her cheeks but lent a sparkle to her eyes that was mistaken for happiness, excitement. She drove herself in the office, rearranging files that were already in perfect order, cleaning desk drawers that had always been neat. She knew David attributed her industry to a desire to have her office in order for her replacement while she was on her honeymoon.

The very word *honeymoon,* which she was beginning to hear more and more frequently in teasing tones, was enough to send a tiny flutter—of what? Fear—up her spine. And she was tired. Lord, was she tired.

Tara looked forward to Thanksgiving as to an oasis in the desert. Although she would be spending most of the day with Alek, she hoped that, surrounded by family, she would be able to rest, relax, be herself. *It seems,* she told herself at the end of the day, *that fools never learn.*

The arrangements were for her and Alek to have the traditional Thanksgiving dinner at one o'clock with her family then, in early evening, go on to his parents' for a cold buffet. Alene and Peter had invited a few close friends to join them, Sallie and David included.

Tara was blissfully alone in the kitchen Thanksgiving morning, humming to herself as she prepared vegetables for a salad, when Alek's soft voice stalked across the room to her from the kitchen doorway.

"Good morning, my love. Happy Thanksgiving."

As Tara jerked around from the sink with a startled "Oh," the paring knife she'd been using slipped from her fingers and bounced around on the floor tiles, dangerously close to her ankles.

"Careful!"

Alek was across the room in three long strides, his hand outstretched to grasp her arm and pull her away.

"Are you hurt? Did it hurt you? Why the hell did you let go of it?"

The sharp, staccato questions struck her like blows and, feeling attacked, she answered defensively, "I—I ... you startled me."

He bent, retrieved the knife with his free hand, dropped it into the sink, then turned her into his arms, holding her loosely.

"That is the second time you nearly injured yourself because, as you say, I startled you. Tara," he said probing gently, "what is it about me that unnerves you so? Are you afraid of me?"

How could she answer him? She didn't know the answers anymore. She felt confused, uncertain. Oh, why had she started this? She was afraid of him. But why? And did he really think she'd ever admit it?

Shaking her head in negation, she said, lying, "Don't be silly. I was deep in thought and—"

"You won't let me near you, will you?" he sighed. "You're hiding behind that invisible fortress you've built around yourself. Tara, don't you realize that while you're locking me out, you're also locking yourself in?"

She didn't want to listen to any more. Making a move to turn out of his arms, she snapped, "I don't know what you're talking about. Now go away so I can finish the salad."

His arms tightened, refusing to let her go. Bending his head, he whispered, "You didn't return my greeting."

"I—"

"But that's all right, I prefer a silent one anyway."

His mouth caught hers, locking on firmly. Tara steeled herself to remain passive then felt a jolt in the pit of her stomach as his lips forced hers apart, demanding a response. Panic crawled through her when she felt the tip of his tongue, and her hands pushed against his chest. He reacted by dropping his hands to her hips, pulling her roughly against him. The hard muscles of his thighs pressed against her urgently.

Her resistance weakened, and as her mouth grew softer, his became harder, bolder. She felt floaty, light-headed, and, her breath quickening in unison with his, her arms snaked up around his neck and clung.

Tightening his arms, he drew her even closer, his hands moving gently along her spine, pressing her softness against the long, hard length of his body. Thought disappeared and was replaced by sensations. The golden curtain dropped around them, and she felt a strange contentment seep through her. For the first time in weeks she felt safe, secure. Sighing softly, she allowed her lips to be parted yet farther, wanting to drown in the firm sweetness of his mouth.

The slamming of the front door reverberated through her like shock waves, setting off an alarm in her mind. Her father's voice, chastising Karl for letting it slam, brought both shame and reason. What did she think she was doing? Was her mind slipping? Was a soldier ever so weary, he sought rest in the camp of his enemy?

With a small cry of self-disgust she backed away from him, eyes closed in pain, her hand covering her quivering lips.

"Tara?"

Shaking her head wildly, she turned away. "Don't say anything."

"Tara, this is ridiculous. If you'd—"

"No! You make me sick. I make myself sick." She spun around to face him, eyes wide, frightened, refusing to see the almost desperate expression in his eyes, to hear the almost pleading note in his voice. "You can go to—you can go to the living room. Keep my father company while I make the salad."

She had been speaking softly, tremulously. Now her tone went hard: "Go away, Alek."

He started toward her then stopped as the kitchen door was pushed open. Marlene's voice preceded her into the room.

"You should have come to church with us, Tara—" On seeing Alek she paused, hands behind her back as she tied an apron around her still slim waist. "Oh! Good morning, Alek. Happy Thanksgiving. I swear, if it wasn't for the mouth-watering smell of that turkey in the oven, I wouldn't believe it was Thanksgiving, it is so mild outside. Why—" She stopped, eyes swinging from Tara to Alek then back to Tara, suddenly feeling the tension that danced between the two. "Is"—she paused, wet her lips—"is anything wrong?"

At the look of anxiety that had replaced the happy glow on her mother's face, Tara caught herself up sharply. Marshaling her rioting emotions, she managed a shaky laugh.

"Of course not, Mama. I was just trying to chase Alek into the living room to Dad, so I can get on with the salad."

Tara saw, but refused to let register, the small sigh Alek expelled before he turned a composed, warm face to her mother.

"Hello, Marlene. Happy Thanksgiving." He had been using her parents' Christian names, at their request, for several days now, yet each time he addressed one of them, Tara felt an uncomfortable twinge. He did it so easily, so effortlessly, as if he'd known and liked them for years.

"I suppose," he went on teasingly, "that if I want to taste said bird in the oven, I had better retreat to the living room, and Herman, as graciously as possible. And you were right. The aroma is mouth-watering. If you've taught Tara all your little kitchen secrets, I'm afraid I'll have to watch my waistline very carefully after we're married."

Tara's fingers curled into her palms, the nails digging into her flesh as she watched her mother's expression change from worry to flushed pleasure. He had completely captivated her mother. Had in fact captivated every member of her family. Betsy became all flustered and pink-cheeked whenever he favored her with one of his teasing, devastatingly gentle smiles. Her brothers trailed around behind him as if in the wake of some vaulted, invincible hero, their expressions bordering on awe. And her father! That was the kicker. Her father walked around with his chest expanded, eyes bright with pride, whenever Alek slipped and called him *sir* instead of *Herman*.

Their attitude, the whole situation, filled Tara with disgust. *They acted as if he were one of the lords of the earth*, she had thought scathingly several times, rather then the devious, arrogant, tyrannical boss he in fact was. Not once did she question her own deeply ingrained opinion of him. He was the enemy. Period.

Tara spent the rest of the day in cold resentment; he had ruined the holiday for her. By the time they reached his parents' home, her resentment had changed to simmering anger. His possessive attitude, his endearments, had her fighting the urge to hit him.

Alene had planned a casual evening and, after the cold buffet supper had been cleared away, they gathered in the living room. As there were more people than chairs, Tara sat on the floor between Alek's and Peter's chairs. The conversation ran the gamut from fashion to politics, becoming more lively when Women's Lib was mentioned.

Tara was just beginning to relax and enjoy herself when Alek's hand dropped onto her shoulder and his cool voice drawled, "I wonder if most women really know what they want?" His eyes rested briefly on his mother's face, then he added, "The most contented women I know are the ones who realize their happiness stems from being well cared for and cherished by the men they belong to."

The overbearing beast! Red flares exploded inside Tara's head. Trembling in anger, she turned her head to stare pointedly at his hand before lifting her head to give him the full blast of fury in her eyes. To keep from shouting Tara had to push her words through her teeth.

"If a slave is your secret desire, Alek, count me out. I will be a slave for no man."

Alek's face paled and, in soothing tones, he murmured, "Tara, I didn't mean—"

"I have reason to know," Tara interrupted bitingly, "you mean exactly what you say. *Belonging to* means ownership and ownership of a human being means slavery. I am, and intend to remain, my own person. With or without your approval. And will you please remove your hand."

. Tara's last words were spoken so cuttingly, Alek snatched his hand away as if he'd been burned. A tide of red crawled across his cheeks, and his eyes held an unfamiliar look of humiliation.

A deathly silence covered the room for some minutes, then Peter's quiet voice eased the tension.

"You deserved that, son," he said easily. "Strangely enough, your mother put me in my place much the same way forty years ago."

"And hard as it may be to believe, Tara," Alene chimed in laughingly, "Peter was even more cocky then Alek."

Her teasing gibe relieved the strain in the room, and everyone began talking at once. Even so, Alek did not touch her for the remainder of the evening.

By the Saturday before the wedding Tara was bewildered and near tears. She couldn't or wouldn't understand her own emotions any longer, and she felt depressed and somehow scared. That afternoon she sat doing her nails, nibbling at her lower lip. There was to be yet another—the last of many—party that night at the home of a lawyer friend of Alek's. From what she had gleaned from Sallie, it was to be a large one, some forty or so guests. This was to be the first really formal party for them, and Tara had shopped for hours till she found the right dress. The fact that her beautiful future mother-in-law would be there was an added spur to her choice. Alene had exquisite taste and always looked as if she had just stepped out of the pages of a haute couture magazine. Also Alek had told her she'd be meeting his cousin Theo at this party, as he was arriving Saturday morning.

The gown was of flame-colored chiffon in the caftan style, free-flowing and sensuous, molding the lines of her figure as she moved, revealing one moment, concealing the next. It was edged in silver braid that in the light reflected onto her hair, giving it a silvery sheen.

As she walked into the living room that evening, she was glad she'd taken more care than usual with her appearance. Alek, in black evening wear, was a devastating threat to any female's senses, and Tara felt her heartbeat quicken. The glittering, sapphire gaze he slowly ran over her didn't help her breathing any, and she drew a deep, calming breath when he murmured, "We had better be going," and turned his eyes away from her to say good night to her parents.

In the car Tara was quiet, her mouth and throat felt dry as bone, and she admitted to herself that she was scared. Tonight, for the first time, she would be meeting Alek's more important friends, and she was naturally anxious.

As he turned the car into the private drive leading to his friends' home, Alek slanted her a sharp glance, then, as if he had been monitoring her thoughts, said gently, "They're only people, you know. Very little different from other people. Some may have more money, some more intelligence, and most, more ambition and drive. But people, just the same. I doubt there'll be a woman there more lovely or poised than you. I wonder sometimes if you fully realize how beautiful and desirable you are." He parked the car in the midst of dozens of others, then turned to face her fully. "Chin up, my sweet. Let's have one of those heart-stopping smiles of yours," he teased.

Feeling a soothing warmth flow through her, Tara did smile, if a little tremulously. Bending his head, he brushed his mouth across hers and whispered, "Now go in there and knock their socks off."

132

The house was very large, very imposing, and more than a little daunting. As they entered the large, impressive hall, Tara unconsciously straightened her shoulders and lifted her head, completely unaware, as she walked into the room full of people, that she had the graceful bearing of a young queen.

Her first impressions were of lights and sounds and colors. The room was brightly lit, the light reflecting even more light as it struck fiery, rainbow-colored sparks off the jewelry that adorned the throats, wrists, fingers, and earlobes of the brilliantly gowned women. The sound was a blend of laughing voices and muted background music coming from several speakers positioned at different spots in the room.

She was vaguely aware of Alek introducing her to her host and hostess, John and Adele Freeland, and they in turn were introducing her to the people standing closest to them. In amazement Tara heard herself responding in a tone of cool self-assurance. Then the press of people separated her from Alek, and what little confidence Tara had, left her completely. She was beginning to feel panic rise when, on a sigh of sheer relief, she saw Alek's father making his way to her through the crowd.

"Good evening, my dear." Peter Rykovsky's voice was a warm caress to badly fraying nerves. Without so much as a by-your-leave he took her cold fingers in his warm hand and said imperviously, "I've been ordered by my lady to bring this delectable young thing to her, and, as you know, Alene's wish is my command."

Warm laughter followed them as he led her adroitly through the milling people, not stopping until Tara stood directly in front of Alene. "Ah, there

133

you are, darling," Alene's lovely voice greeted her. "Come meet my nephew Theo."

Tara turned and felt the breath catch in her throat. Standing next to Alene was a young man who could easily have posed for at least a half dozen Greek statues. His face and form were classically beautiful; his dark, curly hair appeared sculpted to his head; and his eyes were clear and blue as a summer sky. Even, white teeth flashed as he smiled at her and in a voice that held only a hint of an accent he said, "All my life I've secretly thought that Alek was not only the shrewdest but also the luckiest devil alive. Now my beliefs are confirmed. I think I've fallen in love on sight. I don't suppose, beautiful creature, you'd care to run away with me this minute and leave old Alek at the altar, would you?"

In speechless confusion Tara heard Alene's laughing comment and Peter's dry retort. *This young man was almost as outrageous as Alek*, Tara thought. What surprises would the rest of the family have for her?

She was saved from answering him as Sallie joined their small circle, and once again she was being led away. They had taken only a few steps when she had to stop short, her path being barred by an exotically lovely woman whose black eyes glittered maliciously at her. In a tone of barely controlled fury, she purred icily, "I haven't yet met the bride-to-be, Sallie."

A flicker of alarm touched Tara's spine at the hostility underlying the woman's tone, and she looked at her sharply. She was of average height, voluptuously built, with full breasts, a small waist, and full hips that tapered to long, slender legs. Her skin was olive-toned, and right now a dusky pink tinged her cheeks.

Hair as shiny black as sealskin lay smooth and sleek against her head in a short cap-cut. Beautifully arched black brows set off snapping black eyes, which were surrounded by long black lashes. The almond shape of her eyes added to the exotic look of her. The feeling of alarm grew stronger at Sallie's obvious reluctance to introduce them. After what seemed like a long pause Sallie said hurriedly, "Tara Schmitt— Kitty Davenport."

Kitty! *More like the jungle cat*, Tara thought as she acknowledged the introduction. Her thought was proved correct with the woman's next words: "I hope you're enjoying yourself now," she purred. "It won't be long before the novelty of innocence wears off for Alek, and then your nights will be very cold and long."

"Kitty!" Sallie's voice held shocked reproof, even though she'd managed to keep it at a normal tone. Grasping Tara's arm, she drew her away from the nasty laugh that broke from Kitty's dark-red lips. When they were a few feet away from her, Tara whispered, "What was that all about?"

Sallie began to shake her head, then paused and finally said, "I may as well tell you. You'll find out sooner or later anyway." Still grasping her arm, she drew her into a relatively quiet corner, glanced around, then said softly, "Until a few months ago Kitty was Alek's—uh—girl friend. She has been vocally bitter about their breakup. I can't imagine why she was invited to this party."

The searing stab of pain that tore through Tara at Sallie's words stunned her, and she turned her head to hide her pain-filled eyes. She was jealous! Fiercely, hotly jealous, and the knowledge of it frightened and confused her. As if looking for a lifeline, she glanced around the room frantically, and her glance was caught, held by a glittering blue one. Even across the width of the large room Tara saw Alek's eyes grow sharp, questioning. As her eyes stared into that sapphire blaze, a small voice cried out inside, *Dear God, no. No, no, no. I can't, I won't be in love with him.... But you are* came a silent taunt.

Remember how he's hurt you, what he is, she told that silent voice, then she deliberately turned back to Sallie and said coldly, "Girl friend? You mean *mistress,* don't you? Did he pay for an apartment for her in his building or did she just share his?" It was a futile effort to reject her emotions. The pain and humiliation grew to the dimensions of torture, and she was only vaguely aware of the concern in Sallie's voice. "Oh, Tara, does it really matter? It was over months ago."

Yes, Tara thought. *But for how long?* How long would it be before Alek, once having acquired the one thing he'd been denied, became bored and began looking around for a diversion? And Kitty would be there in his sight; of that Tara felt quite sure.

CHAPTER EIGHT

Tara opened her eyes the morning of her wedding and closed them again quickly, tightly. The weather matched her emotional condition. The sky was weeping hard, and although Tara's eyes were now dry, inside her heart the tears fell as swiftly as the raindrops. The days she lived through since the party—a week ago tonight—had been pure hell.

Vainly and painfully she had fought against the realization of her love for Alek. She had spent as little time with him as possible, telling him she had too much to do. His skeptical eyes questioned her, although he didn't voice his doubts. She went to her apartment several evenings, ostensibly to pack her things for removal to Alek's apartment, only to pace from room to room crying bitter tears. She didn't want to love him. She didn't even want to like him.

What was she to do? The desire to make him pay for what he'd done to her had been cauterized by that searing knife of jealousy on Saturday night. She hurt badly yet she knew, somehow, that the pain she now knew was nothing to what would come later. Twice she had left the apartment to go back to her parents, firmly determined to tell them she could not go through with the wedding. Both times the words died on her lips at the sight of her mother's face.

The rehearsal last night had been an ordeal that was not helped by Theo's light banter. When it had finally been over, Alek had led Tara outside to his car, brushing aside her protested "Alek, my car," with a curt "I'll bring you back for it."

He had not driven far, parking the car again on a dimly lighted street. Resting an arm on the steering wheel, he slanted a long look at her before asking tightly, "Last-minute jitters, Tara? You've been withdrawn and jumpy all week. Is something wrong? Aren't you feeling well?"

"I feel fine," she murmured, twisting her hands in her lap. "I'm a little tired, that's all."

He turned to face her fully, his one long hand covering hers stilled their agitated movement. Head bent, Tara studied his slim-fingered hand, felt its warmth seep into her cold skin. A small shiver rippled along her spine as his hand moved, slid up her arm to grasp her shoulder. "Look at me, Tara."

When she didn't comply at once, he released her shoulder and caught her chin in his fingers, lifting her head and turning her face to his descending mouth. She forced herself to remain passive, silently fighting down the tingling in her fingers, the warmth spreading through her body. Feeling somehow that if she didn't break contact with his persuading mouth, she'd be lost forever, she pulled her lips away from his with a small sob.

"Alek, please take me home. I'm very tired, and isn't Theo having a bachelor party for you tonight?"

"Yes he is, but there's no hurry." His fingers caressed her cheek, brushed lightly at the few strands of silky hair that had fallen across her face. His mouth followed the progress of his hand and, as his fingers slid into the deep waves of her hair, his lips, close to her ear, whispered, "Only one more day, pansy eyes, and this mad rushing around will be over. You can rest then, and I'll help you. The medicine I've got for you works better than any tranquilizer ever made." Then his mouth found hers again, hard, demanding a response from her. Trembling, breathless, she could feel her resistance slipping away, and in desperation she brought her hands up to his head and pushed him away. "Alek, don't."

He flung himself back behind the steering wheel, breathing hard, smoldering, darkened eyes roaming her face.

"You're right," he rasped. "I'd better take you home before I decide the hell with the party and take you to my place." He paused then added roughly, "I want you badly, Tara. Tomorrow can't come soon enough."

Now, lying in her bed, Tara groaned aloud at the memory and turned her face into the pillow. Why hadn't she backed out of this days ago, as soon as she'd felt that soul-destroying stab of jealousy? She wanted to run away and hide, and it was too late. Within a few hours she would be his wife. His words, like a scratched record, kept repeating in her head. *"I want you badly." I want you. Want. Want. Want.*

The rain still poured from leaden skies when Tara, pale, ethereal, and unknowingly beautiful, was dressed and ready to leave for the church. A bubble of hysterical laughter caught then lodged in her throat at the incongruity of tugging clear plastic boots over her white satin slippers and carefully

139

catching her long, full skirt around her knees, under the protective rain cape her father placed around her shoulders. From house to car, from car to church, George held a large golf umbrella over her.

The feeling of unreality that had gripped Tara from the minute she'd begun dressing mushroomed and grew until now, poised, ready to follow Betsy down the aisle, she felt cold, numb. The signaling organ chord was struck, her father's shoulder nudged hers, and she moved in measured step beside him, unaware of the several small gasps or open stares of admiration that greeted her appearance.

The gown Tara had chosen was of white satin, starkly beautiful in its simplicity. It fit snugly from the high collar that encircled her throat to the nipped-in waist, and from her shoulders to where the sleeves ended in a V point on the back of her hands at the middle fingers. From the waist the skirt belled out full and voluminous, ending in a short train in back. It was completely without adornment of either fabric or jewelry.

In a strangely withdrawn state Tara walked slowly down the long aisle, drawing ever nearer to the two cousins, both handsome in different ways. They watched her progress with different expressions: Theo's smile was soft, his eyes warmly appreciating her beauty. Alek's unsmiling countenance was held in, taut, expressionless. His eyes blazed with a fierce possessiveness, and something Tara couldn't define.

The withdrawn, cold state lasted throughout most of the ceremony, and not until the blessing was being given did Tara feel the first pangs of guilt. She had agreed to marry this man for a very unholy reason.

Revenge. In any way that presented itself, she had decided to make him pay for what he'd done to her. The fact that his reason—lust—was equally sinful didn't matter. The fact that she now loved him didn't excuse her either. She was in the house of God and she was committing a reprehensible act; she felt, if possible, more miserable than before.

Finally it was all over. Not just the ceremony, but the picture-taking as well. And now the hand that tugged the plastic boots over her slippers felt weighted from the heavy, wide gold band Alek had slid onto her finger. And the car that whisked them to the Hotel Traylor for the reception was shared by her husband.

She was thankful for the numbed coldness that had enveloped her again during the long period of picture-taking, and it carried her through the reception. A smile cramping her neck and jaw muscles, she went through the motions of the leadoff dance, the cake-cutting, and the tossing of the bouquet, all the while blinking at the incessant flash of light from the hired photographer. On the point of thinking it would go on forever, Tara felt the firm clasp of Alek's hand and walked beside him as he made a determined move to the door.

The plan had been for them to change clothes at Alek's—now their—apartment, then go on to New York for a week. It had grown colder, and the rain still slashed against the windshield. After Alek had maneuvered the car into the steady stream of late-afternoon traffic, he said abruptly, "I wouldn't be a bit surprised if this rain turns to snow in a little while. We're not driving to New York in this tonight, we'll wait and leave in the morning."

141

At the sound of finality in his tone, Tara gulped back the protest forming on her lips, her panic at the prospect of being alone with him that much sooner closing her throat to speech.

His apartment, in a fairly new modern complex, was large and luxurious. Tara had been in it once before, on Thursday night, when they had transported her clothes from her father's house. She had been given the grand tour of: Alek's large bedroom and a smaller one, both with their own baths; a roomy, well-equipped kitchen and cozy dining area; and a huge living room, part of which had been sectioned off as a bar area. The furnishings were Scandinavian modern, the lines straight and clean, yet overall the impression was one of the kind of comfort that comes only with money.

Alek turned the key in the lock, pushed the door open, reached inside to flick on the light switch, then ushered Tara in, saying dryly, "I think I'll save the over-the-threshold tradition until we move into a home of our own, if you don't mind."

Tara shook her head and walked into the room, only to stop and glance around irresolutely. The sound of the door being closed softly, the click of the lock springing into place, set her in motion, and she hurried toward the bedroom, her voice breathless. "I—I think I'll change. The bottom of my gown got wet and it's heavy and uncomfortable."

She dashed into the bedroom, closed the door behind her, and leaned weakly against it, gasping for air. Dear Lord, what was she going to do? She didn't think she could face him again, yet she was trapped inside this apartment with him. Moving away from the door, she walked around the room nervously, her eyes not registering the light-wood tone of the double dresser, the chest of drawers, the desk, the big over-stuffed chair covered in pale green tweed, the deep rich green of carpeting and draperies or pristine white of walls, ceiling, and woodwork. But mostly her eyes avoided the wide double bed with its coverlet in a bold, dark-green-and-white geometric design.

Without thinking, her trembling fingers slid open the zippers on the inside of her sleeves, moved to tug at the long one that ran from the back of her neck to her waist. She managed to get it halfway down, then no amount of stretching or reaching would move it an inch farther. In agitated frustration, Tara tugged on her sleeves, hoping to slip the gown off her shoulders, enabling her to twist the zip around to the front. She was on the verge of tears when the bedroom door opened and Alek asked softly, "Need any help?"

"I can't get the damned zipper down," she cried irritably and heard his low laugh as he came across the room to her. She felt his fingers at her back, then the zip was sliding easily to its base. A pause, then his hands parted the material, slid inside and around her waist, scorching her skin through the thin fabric of her slip. As if his fingers actually burned her, she jerked away from him.

"Alek, I'd like to take a shower." Trembling, she turned to face him, a plea in her eyes. "Please."

His eyes glowed darkly as they roved over her body then came back to study her face. "That is a strikingly beautiful gown." His voice was a blatant caress, rippling over her skin like warm satin. "It almost does you justice. All right, my sweet, have your shower. I'll use the other bathroom and take one too." Then his voice sounded a mild warning note.

"You have exactly one half hour." With that he calmly walked to the closet, yanked out a long dark-brown hooded robe, and sauntered out of the room.

Tara released her tensely held breath on a long sigh then quickly removed her gown and underthings, tossing the lot onto the overstuffed chair. Plunging her hand into the closet, she grabbed the long white satin robe she'd hung there Thursday night and ran into the chocolate-brown-and-white-tiled bathroom. Impatiently she twisted and pinned up her almost waist-long hair, shrugging at the short, curly neck hairs that escaped the shower cap she pulled onto her head. Standing under the hot, stinging spray, she longed for a few extra minutes to stand and let the fingerlike jets work the tenseness out of her body. But she didn't have a few extra minutes, for she had made up her mind to dress and leave the apartment before Alek finished his shower.

In fumbling haste she dried her body, slipped into her robe, and scrubbed her teeth. Her hair a silver-blond mass of waves rioting over her shoulders and down her back, she pulled open the bathroom door, stepped through it, and stopped cold at the sound of Alek's sharply indrawn breath.

He was standing just inside the bedroom door as if he'd just that minute entered. The robe hung to the top of his bare feet, the belt looped tightly around his lean waist, the hood lay loosely on his back.

Tara stood motionless, as if mesmerized. His softly spoken words, as he moved toward her, startled her into awareness. "God, Tara, you're beautiful."

Cautiously she moved away from him, toward the far-window wall, her voice sounding hoarse and strained to her ears. "This is a mistake. I can't stay here, Alek. I'd like you to leave the room so I can dress. I'm going home."

He paused, then continued to her, stopping a foot in front of her. In growing alarm she watched his face harden, his eyes change from confusion to wariness to anger.

"Like hell I'll leave this room." She flinched at the whip-flick cutting sting of his voice. "If there's been a mistake, you made it and you'll live with it, and me. You're not going anywhere. You *are* home."

Shrinking inside at the coldness of his tone, Tara drew a deep breath and, moving quickly, she circled around him and made for the door. Her hair was her undoing, for as she swung away from him, it fanned out and around her head. With lightning swiftness his arm shot out, and he caught a handful, making her cry out with the pain that stung her scalp. He gave a tug to turn her around to him and she lost her balance and crashed to the floor on her knees in front of him. Giving another sharp tug he jerked her head back, turned her face up to the cold, hard planes of his. Through tightly clenched teeth he growled, "You're my wife, Tara, and you'll stay my wife. I've waited long enough; I'll wait no longer."

Defiance blazed out of her eyes and in an attempt to inflict pain on him, as he was on her, she flashed, "You're a savage. Underneath that thin veneer of civilization you're as wild and unruly as a marauding cossack. A savage, do you hear?"

His glittering blue eyes never leaving hers, he dropped onto his knees in front of her. "I hear," he rasped. "And this evening, my love, you are going to find out what it feels like to be made love to by a savage."

His mouth crushed hers, then his head jerked back, and she watched in horrified fascination as a drop of blood formed and grew at the wound in his lip her biting teeth had inflicted. His tongue flicked out, removed the blood, which was replaced at once with another drop. Alek lowered his head slowly to her again and, his lips almost touching hers, he whispered, "And you call me a savage?" Then with cool deliberation he caught her lip between his teeth and bit hard. His mouth covering hers smothered her outcry and she tasted the salty flavor of his blood. Or was it hers?

With all her concentration centered on remaining passive, unaffected by the disturbing pressure of his mouth, Tara was only vaguely aware of his fingers relaxing, sliding away from her hair. His other arm was around her tightly, pinning both of hers to her side. Slowly he began to move, sideways and down, drawing her with him. His free hand braced on the floor, he lowered them both to the soft pile carpeting, his lips still locked on hers.

Turning her at the last moment, her back hit the floor with a dull thud at the same time his hard chest struck hers, knocking the wind out of her. Feeling suffocated, Tara managed to turn her head away from him, gasping for air. Not once breaking contact, his lips slid across her soft cheek to her ear, and she uttered a tiny gasp when his teeth nibbled at her lobe.

"Tara, I don't want to force you." Tara shivered at the impassioned whisper. "But this marriage will be consummated tonight. I *will* make you mine. Never have I wanted to own a woman the way I want to own you. Don't fight me, love, or, in different ways, you'll hurt us both."

Fleetingly she wondered at the meaning of his words, then all thought fled, for his lips were sending small tongues of flame into every vein in her body. With tiny, devastating kisses his lips moved from her ear to the corner of her mouth where, along with the tip of his tongue, he teased and tantalized until every one of her senses cried out with the need to feel those lips, that tongue, against her own.

"Alek."

His name broke from her throat with a small sob as she moved her head the fraction of an inch needed to slide her mouth under his. She heard the breath catch in his throat, as if in disbelief, then his mouth crushed hers more savagely than before, in an excitingly desperate kind of way, plundering, seeking every ounce of sweetness there.

It seemed the whole world was on fire, and she was the very center of the blaze. Filled with a sudden, urgent need to touch him, her hands broke free of his imprisoning hold and, parting the lapels of his robe, she slid her hands across his chest, exhilaration singing through her when she felt him shudder at her touch.

With a groan his mouth left hers and he buried his face in the curve of her neck, his hand brushing her robe aside roughly. She felt his warm breath tickle her skin, heard again the same incomprehensible Russian words he'd spoken before. Moving quickly, he lifted her and removed her robe, then shed his own, his eyes scorching her body as they roved slowly over her.

Having him away from her, even that short distance, brought a measure of sanity. What was she doing? She had to stop this. But she loved him so.

Needed him so. Two tears escaped over the edge of her lower lids and rolled slowly across her cheeks into her hair. Instantly he was beside her, his hands cupping her face.

"Tara, darling, don't be frightened."

Frightened? Yes, she was frightened of her own response, of the overwhelming longing to be close to him, belong to him.

Dropping tiny, fiery kisses, his lips surveyed her face while his hands caressed and aroused her body. His softly murmured words added fuel to the rapidly spreading flames inside her.

Moaning softly, she curled her arms tightly around his neck, gave up her mouth in total surrender. Somewhere in the deep recess of her mind she knew she'd have to pay for it for the rest of her life. Yesterday was over. Tomorrow was far away. The only thing that held any meaning for her was here, and now, and him. The apartment, the city, the world dissolved, and it was as if they were alone on a tiny island, soaring through time and space.

His hard body moved over hers, and his lips close to her ear whispered, "I must hurt you, love, but I promise you the pain will not last long, and it will set you free. Free to give me as much or as little as you wish. Free to accept everything I have to offer."

On his last words pain ripped through the lower part of her body and, stiffening with outrage and shock, she arched away from him, the cry of rejection that tore from her lips drowning inside his mouth. With infinite patience and surprising restraint he kissed, caressed, soothed her tension-contracted body until the pain receded and was replaced by a fierce urgency inside her to know a oneness with him.

The gentle appeaser was gone with her first renewed stirrings, replaced by a hard, demanding lover, intent on fulfillment. When he exploded off the edge of their tiny island in space, he took her with him. Shuddering, gasping for breath, for one small moment she seemed to face the pure white light of the sun, then she went spiraling through the darkness of space, held softly, securely, within the steellike coils of his arms. If someone had told Tara one week, one day ago, that surrendering herself completely to Alek would fill her with such ecstasy, she would never have believed it, as much as she loved him. This beauty and contentment that engulfed every part of her being were part of the make-believe used in romantic literature and films. The idea that all the passion that ever poured out of the pen of poets or lyricists had to be based in some fact had never occurred to her.

Slowly the awareness of time and place crept back to her. She felt the soft carpet against her skin, the night-cooled air in the room lightly cooling her flesh. She felt Alek's thumping heart return to a normal beat, heard his ragged breathing grow more even. Still held tightly against his hard body, she felt his breath stir her hair as he whispered in an almost awed tone, "Never in all my wildest fantasizing have I dreamed that anything could be so perfect." His arms tightened possessively and his mouth covered hers in a deep consuming kiss. When he lifted his head, his voice was firm, though still soft. "The marriage has been consummated in three ways, Tara. With the mingling of our blood, the joining of our bodies, and the coupling of our souls. If what we've just experienced is savagery, then I give up all claims to civilization."

Tara slept, then was jarred awake again when Alek lifted her from the floor and carried her to the bed. It seemed very late and she was shivering; goose bumps covered her arms and shoulders. He left her a moment and the room was plunged into darkness. Then he was back, sliding onto the bed next to her, drawing the covers up and around them before pulling her into his arms hard against him.

"I'm so cold." The words trembled from her lips shakily.

"I know. I'm sorry. I fell asleep. I haven't slept that deeply since I was a child."

His murmured words were revealing something of importance to her, but the deeper meaning of them was lost to her sleep-hazy mind.

Slowly, as warmth returned to her body, heat returned to his, and within minutes he was whispering her name between fierce, demanding kisses, his hands possessive, his body pressing hers into the mattress urgently.

If she'd have thought, she would have believed it impossible to experience that same oneness as before. Yet if anything, their wild, explosive flight through space this time ended in a more perfect unity. More slowly, languorously, she drifted back to an awareness of Alek's mouth lazily branding small kisses over her face, her throat, her shoulders, and lingeringly, her breasts. Sighing in deep contentment, she was beyond wondering at the strangely fervent tone of his voice, or the meaning of the oft repeated Russian words. Almost purring, she curled against him like a well-petted kitten, her fingers idly stroking his muscle-ridged back. One minute she felt more vibrantly alive than ever before in her life, and in the next, sensuously drowsy, she slipped into a deep, relaxed sleep.

The early-morning rays of sun touching Tara's face wakened her. Closing her eyes again quickly, she moved to roll onto her side and grew still, suddenly aware of a weight on her chest. Turning her head slowly, she opened her eyes and stared at Alek sprawled beside her, one arm flung across her breasts.

Memory returned in a flash, and she felt the hot string of tears behind her lids. Afraid to move, barely breathing, her eyes roved over him lovingly. The covers were twisted about his slim waist, leaving his broad shoulders and chest exposed to the chill air in the room. Slowly she curled her fingers into her palm, fighting down the urge to touch, to slide her fingers over his smooth skin, to feel the curly spring of dark hair tickle her palm.

Eyes moving slowly, missing nothing, trailed up to the strong column of his throat and rested a moment on the steady pulsebeat there. Her throat closing with emotion, she lifted her eyes to his head. Silky black waves were tousled, one swath lying endearingly across his forehead, and Tara felt a pang remembering it was her fingers that had caused the disorder. Long, thick, inky lashes threw shadows onto his high cheekbones, the lines of which, along with his firm jaw, were somewhat softened in sleep. Her eyes rested on his beautifully chiseled mouth; her lips ached with the need to kiss him.

Her lashes glistened with tears; consumed with the desire to wake him, to beg him to hold her close, she tore her eyes away and stared at the ceiling. Her mind working furiously, Tara tried to find an alternative to what she knew she must do. Finally her lids closed in defeat. It was no good. It would never be any good. And she knew it. Her heart cried at the realization, but she knew she couldn't stay with him. Gone were the vaguely formed plans to make him pay for what he'd done to her. Before, she'd been angry, hurt. Now she was terrified.

Why did the night have to end? she thought bitterly. Why had she slept and wasted so much of it? He had been so gentle, then so demanding, his hands and mouth awaking a sleeping tiger of passion she had never dreamed she possessed. She shivered with remembrances, then her eyes flew open. What must he think of her now? She didn't even want to think about that, so she pushed the thought aside, then felt a shaft of blinding pain as a new consideration slithered its way into her mind. His love-making had been so completely mind-shattering. It had affected her two ways, physically and mentally, striking to the very core of her being. She had known she was in love with him for some days; now she belonged to him. What would it be like to be actually loved by him?

The thought drove the pain deeper, and she stirred restlessly. There was the cause of her misery, the reason she could not stay with him. For he did not love her. What had his words been? She had no need to ask herself the question, for she could hear his voice as if it had been yesterday: *"If the only way I can have you is through marriage, I'll marry you."*

Just in time Tara caught back the sob that rose in her throat. If she stayed with him now, slept with him, he'd crush her spirit and independence. Loving him so deeply, she'd be like clay in his hands. His nearness made her ache; his touch set her on fire. Her dependence on him would grow, and within a short amount of time he could make a near-slave of her. And being the epitome of dominance, he would relish the enslavement. She would end hating herself and probably him also.

No, no, no, she told herself. She would not, she could not, let that happen. She must end it, now, this morning.

As if it were a sign, he moved in his sleep, lifting his arm from her and flinging it back over his head. She was free and with a shiver she slid her naked body off the bed. Their robes lay in a heap where he had tossed them last night and, scooping hers up, she slipped into it and wrapped it around her slim form, tying the belt securely.

Like a sleepwalker she moved to stand at the windows, staring down at the Sunday morning street empty of traffic, her arms wrapped around her trembling body.

"Good morning, pansy eyes. Come back to bed." Alek's sleepy soft voice reached out across the room to envelop her like a caress. "There's something I want to tell you. Something I forgot in the—uh—heat of the moment last night."

Tara shook her head, her fingers biting deeply into her upper arms in an effort to still her increased trembling.

"Tara," he crooned, "this bed is getting colder by the second. It's early yet. Come back here and we'll warm it together."

"No." It sounded like a frog's croak and Tara cleared her throat nervously.

"No, Alek, I'm not coming back to bed with you. Not now. Not ever again."

The silence that blanketed the room had the cold stillness of death. Tara's nails dug unmercifully into her flesh. Why didn't he speak? Swear at her? Anything but this silence that seemed to stretch forever and tear her nerves apart. When he finally did speak, the sound of his voice was as chilling as the silence had been.

"When you speak to me, Tara, please have the courtesy to look at me."

The insolent tone of his words had the same effect on Tara as if he'd smacked her with a cold, wet towel. She spun around, head up, eyes blazing with defiance. The sight of him stole the stinging retort from her lips. He had pushed himself back and up against the pillows, more in a reclining than a sitting position. His long torso, exposed to at least two inches below the navel, had a golden, toast-brown hue in the morning sun. He didn't move or say anything, and yet the invitation was as clear as if he'd held out his arms and whispered, "Come to me."

And she wanted to. With every fiber and particle of her being, she wanted to. She had lain in this man's arms all night. He had opened doors, shown her beauty she had never dreamed existed. For one sharp instant she felt not only willing to be his slave, but longed for it. She actually took one step toward him when her eyes touched his face, and she was stopped cold, pinned to the spot by two rapier-sharp points of glinting blue.

"That's better," he said coolly. "Now what the hell is this all about?"

Tara drew a deep calm breath. Somehow she

had to match his coolness. "Exactly what I said, Alek. I won't sleep with you again." Lord, was that detached voice hers?

"You can say that to me after last night?" Anger ruffled the coolness now. Anger and a touch of disbelief. "Do you have any idea how rare an experience like that is?"

Without realizing it, she was shaking her head. She didn't know, not really, but she was beginning to. So many things that she'd never quite understood began to make sense. "The world well lost for love"—that had always baffled her. The idea that anyone could turn his back on the world, or his own small corner of it, had been beyond her comprehension. Yet now, if he loved her, just a little, she would happily do just that. But he didn't, and the knowledge was tearing her to shreds.

Catching back the urge to put her pain into words, to cry out, "Alek, please love me," she replied hoarsely, "It doesn't matter."

"It doesn't matter?" His words were barely whispered, and yet the astonishment in them had the impact of a shout. His eyes closed briefly, and Tara told herself she misread the emotion she'd glimpsed in them. She knew she did not have the power to hurt him. The truth of this hit her forcefully when he lifted his lids, for his eyes were hard and cold and filled with contempt for her. He moved abruptly to get up and, startled, Tara stepped back, catching a glimpse of his long, muscular thigh before her lids veiled her eyes.

"You can open your eyes now," Alek murmured sardonically a few moments later, then his voice went flat. "Would you care to tell me what you intend to do?"

He had put on his robe, and as Tara opened her eyes, he drew a pack of cigarettes from the pocket. Without asking, he lit one, handed it to her then lit one for himself, squinting at her through the gray smoke. Tara drew deeply on the cigarette, then exhaled slowly before answering equally flatly, "Go back to my apartment. Go back to work. Get a divorce."

"Of course. This is the way you get your revenge. Right?"

His voice was dangerously soft and his eyes watched sharply, through narrowed lids, for her response.

She didn't disappoint him. Swallowing with difficulty she gasped, "You—you knew?"

He sighed almost wearily. "Credit me with at least a little intelligence, Tara. You ran up the white flag too abruptly. Did an about-face too quickly to be believable. I knew at once you were up to something. It took me all of about ninety seconds to come up with the word *revenge*. You had decided to make me pay. My mistake was in thinking you were planning to make me pay through the wallet. I have to admit, you threw me when you refused an engagement ring. But then I decided you were waiting until everything was legal to put the bite on me."

Tara flinched and whispered, "You don't have a very high opinion of me, do you?"

"I pushed you pretty hard," he said quietly. "You were hurt and angry and wanted to retaliate." Shrugging carelessly, he added, "I wanted you and I was willing to pay the price."

His words stung, brought a flush of color to her

cheeks, and she said angrily, "Pay the price? Like I was a common—"

"Don't say it, Tara," he cut in warningly. "That's not true, so don't ever say it." He was quiet a moment, then he asked softly, "Last night wasn't part of the plan, was it?"

Tara wet her lips nervously and slid her eyes away from his, unable to maintain that hard blue contact. "There—there was no actual plan. I just felt I had to make you pay, somehow."

"And now you're going to walk out of this room and out of my life?" She should have been warned by the silky sound of his voice but, in trying to hang on to her own composure, she missed it and answered calmly, "Yes."

"Think again." Startled eyes flew back to his at the finality of his tone. Before she could protest, he went on blandly. "Have you thought what you are going to tell people? Sallie and David? The rest of your friends? The people you work with?" He paused, then underlined: "Your parents. Yesterday you were the picture of a gloriously happy bride. What can you give as a reason for leaving me? That you suddenly fell out of love? Hardly. That I beat you? Where are the marks? That I'm a terrible lover? Well, as everyone was convinced we anticipated our vows anyway, I don't think that will do. So what can you tell them? Can you imagine what your father is going to say?" He paused again before adding ruthlessly, "Or your mother's face?"

Her mother! A low strangled moan escaped Tara's lips. *Dear Lord.* She hadn't thought. Had been too full of thoughts of him to spare any for anything or anyone else. A picture of her mother's face the day before, serenely happy, looking almost young again, formed in front of Tara's eyes. In pain she closed her lids against the image.

Insensitive to her distress, words hard, measured, as if underlined darkly, Alek drove on ruthlessly. "Which, do you think, will be harder for her to take? The *idea* of her daughter sleeping with a man without benefit of clergy or the *fact* of her daughter leaving her husband the day after a full Catholic wedding?"

As he spoke, he walked slowly to her, coming to a stop so close, she could feel his breath on her hair. She kept her eyes tightly closed, vainly trying to control the shudder that ripped through her body at his nearness.

"Look at me, Tara."

It was a command. One, his hard tone warned her, she dared not disobey. Slowly, she lifted her head and her eyelids, then swallowed with difficulty. His eyes were as cold and hard as the stone they matched.

"As I said, you'd better think again. For if you go through with this, I won't make it easy for you. In fact I'll make it very hard. I'll fight you publicly. Make an unholy field day for the newspapers." His voice dropped to a menacing growl. "In short, Tara, I'll tear you apart."

"But why?" Eyes wide with confusion and more than a little fear, Tara's cry was one of despair.

"The Rykovskys do not divorce." Flat, final, the words struck her like blows. "You seem to forget, I also have parents. Who, by the way, love you already. I will not have them hurt."

His hands came up to cradle her face; long brown fingers, unbelievably gentle after his harsh words, brushed at the tears that had escaped her lids and rolled down her morning-shiny cheeks. His voice was now low, husky, yet still firmly determined. "No, Tara. You've made your bed and now we'll lie in it. Together."

"No!" In desperation she jerked away from him. Away from his warm, caressing fingers. Those hard, compelling eyes. That hypnotic, druglike voice that was sapping the resistance from her body. She put the width of the room between them before she turned to face him again, eyes blazing. "I'll stay with you. Play the role of the adoring wife. But I want nothing from you, either material or physical. I will not share your bed." She paused to draw a deep, calming breath, then added quietly, "And if you try and force me, I'll go, and to hell with the consequences."

"Don't do this, Tara." His quiet voice seemed to float on the angry silence left by her bitter words. "We could have a good life together if you'd—"

Weakening, and frightened of it, Tara cut in scathingly, "If only I'd agree to every one of your dictates. Thank you, but no thank you. I've given you my terms, Alek. It's the only way I'll stay."

His face a mask, he studied her a moment, then turned away with a shrug so unconcerned, so indifferent, it sent a shaft of hot pain into Tara's heart.

"Now, if you don't mind, I think we'd better dress." His detached tone deepened Tara's pain. "I'm hungry, and I'd planned to stop for breakfast on the way to New York."

"You still want to go?" she gasped.

He turned back swiftly, eyes hard and cold. "My dear wife, do we have a choice? The reservations are made. Everyone thinks we're there now. Our only other option is to pen ourselves in this apartment for a week. Would you prefer that?"

"No!" Tara answered quickly, then more slowly, "No, of course not. I—I'll be ready in half an hour." As she turned to escape his unyielding stare, his taunting voice stopped her on the threshold. "One more thing, Tara. I'm a normal male, with all the natural drives. I was fully prepared to live up to the vows I made yesterday, as regards fidelity. Your attitude changes that. Do you understand?"

Tara froze, unable to force herself to look back at him, a picture of the smirking Kitty locked in her mind. Fingers like ice, she pulled the door wide and stepped into the hall.

"Do you?" Alek insisted.

"Yes."

It was a hoarse whisper hanging in the air. Tara had fled.

CHAPTER NINE

The following Sunday afternoon Tara sat in a state of bemusement listening to her husband's smooth, quiet voice as it blended with the low hum of the T-bird's engine as they neared home.

It had been a surprisingly relaxing week. Alek had revealed a facet of his character unseen by Tara up till now. He had been courteous and considerate, easygoing and almost light-hearted, as he squired her around New York.

They had walked the city until she thought her legs would drop off, and she doubted there were any elaborate Christmas decorations anywhere that they had not admired. Secretly her favorites were the angels and the enormous tree in Rockefeller Center. They had started early every morning and had gone full tilt until after midnight every night. They had dined at a variety of restaurants, from Lüchow's and Tavern-on-the-Green to Mama Leone's, the Top of the Six's, and even Windows on the World.

One night he took her to a famous disco, surprising her even more on the dance floor with his perfectly executed, somewhat sensuous step. And Tara had to admit to more than a twinge of pride and jealousy at the blatantly admiring female glances cast over his long, slim form clothed in snugly fitting pale gray slacks and sweater over a pin-striped black-and-white shirt.

As they were having breakfast Wednesday morning Tara said suddenly, "Alek, if you don't mind, I'd like to do some shopping today. I haven't finished my Christmas shopping and I think it'd be fun, especially for Mama and Betsy, to receive gifts from New York."

"Why should I mind?" he asked blandly, then added sardonically, "It's your honeymoon too, you know. I'm sure I can amuse myself for a few hours. Where would you like to go? Bloomingdale's? Saks?"

"I don't know. The few times I've been in New York have been on day tours. Just time enough to see a show, squeeze in some sight-seeing. I've never done any shopping here."

"Bloomingdale's," he stated firmly. "If you've never been there, it'll blow your mind."

It did. Tara was fascinated with the store. When she had the time and money, she loved to shop. This morning she had both. When Alek had deposited her at the entrance, he had stuffed a wad of bills into her bag, told her he'd be outside the same entrance at three o'clock, and added dryly, "Have fun."

Three o'clock? she had thought. What in the world was she to do for five hours? Time slipped away easily. At first Tara was content to stroll around aimlessly, delighted with the unusual and varied selection of merchandise. When she finally did get down to serious shopping, she spent long minutes on her choice of gifts for her mother, Betsy, and Sallie, feeling a pang of guilt as the money Alek had given her quickly dwindled.

With her father and brothers in mind, Tara wan

dered into the men's department, growing suddenly taut with an intense longing. It seemed every third article her eyes touched screamed Alek's name at her. Alek was always well groomed, and though Tara knew he had a huge closet full of beautifully tailored clothes, she wanted to buy him everything.

For a few moments, a small smile on her lips, she allowed her thoughts to run riot, picturing low-slung expensive sports cars, sparkling white yachts, sleek-lined Thoroughbreds. Pulling her thoughts up short with a mental shake, she lovingly touched fine-knit cashmere sweaters, beautifully made raw-silk shirts.

On the point of walking away, she stopped. Well, why not? It was Christmastime, wasn't it? The time for buying gifts. Also the excuse she needed. With a determined step she turned back, a happy gleam in her eyes, and promptly lost all sense of time. She bought discriminately but lavishly, this time extracting bills from her own wallet, not caring about the rate of speed with which they disappeared.

Tara could have gone on for hours, but a glimpse of her watch brought her shopping spree to an abrupt halt with a disbelieving gasp. It was a few minutes after three. She was keeping Alek waiting.

Alek's eyebrows rose in amusement when she finally staggered out of the store under the weight of her packages.

"When the lady says she's going to shop, she's going to shop," he teased. "Did you enjoy yourself?"

"Oh, Alek," she replied happily, unaware that for the first time since they'd met, she had responded to him warmly, spontaneously. "I've had a wonderful time and I'm starving."

She missed the quick narrowing of his eyes, his

brief hesitation, for they were gone in a flash, and he was chiding her gently. "Didn't you take time to have lunch?"

"Lunch?" she laughed happily. "I never even thought of food."

Relieving her of the bulk of her burden, he helped her into the cab he had managed to hail and smiled dryly. "In that case I think we can find you a crust of bread and a glass of water somewhere."

After dropping her purchases in their room, Alek led Tara to a small table in the hotel's bar. When he gave the waiter an order of a sandwich and coffee for her and only a drink for himself, she turned questioning eyes to him.

Smiling easily, he murmured, "I didn't forget to eat lunch."

Happy with her day and for the first time in weeks at peace in her own mind, Tara returned his smile with a brilliant one of her own. The waiter appeared at their table at the same moment, and Tara missed the low sound of breath catching in Alek's throat, the fleeting expression of longing, of hunger in his eyes.

At no time during the week had Alek made a move of a physical nature toward her. Other than taking her elbow while crossing streets and occasionally sliding his arm around her waist in extracrowded places, he did not touch her. Every night had been the same. He'd see her to their hotel room then go to the bar for thirty or so minutes to give her time to get into her nightgown and into one of the two double beds in the room.

Now, not more than forty-five minutes from home, the atmosphere in the car was the exact opposite of that of a week ago. Tara sat back comfortably, her bemusement stemming from Alek's homebound conversation. Some stray remark had touched at a memory, and he had been relating anecdotes from his boyhood. It was the first time he'd opened up to her and, at her hesitant query about his ancestors, he'd gone quiet and she was afraid he'd withdrawn again when he resumed his smooth, quiet tone.

"The Rykovskys go back a long way and were, at one time, entertained by the czars. My great-grandparents were uneasy under the rule of Alexander the Third and possibly read the handwriting on the wall. At any rate, they transferred as much of their property as possible into cash and left Russia around 1883, when my grandfather was still quite small. They landed and stayed in Philadelphia for a while, and then a merchant my great-grandfather had met and made friends with invited them to come and visit him in his neck of the woods. That, of course, was the Allentown area. They came, liked what they saw, and settled. My great-grandfather was an intelligent, well-educated man who liked to tinker with machines and tools. After he was settled, he built a small shop and put his hobby to work. Although my grandfather and then my father added to it, the original shop is still there."

"And now you're building a new one," Tara said softly.

"Yes, we've outgrown the old."

Again he was quiet a few moments, then he slanted a glance at her and smiled. "You said once that I have an international family, and in a sense you're right. While doing the grand tour, my grandfather met and eventually married the shy, youngest daughter of a wealthy French wine-producing family. I still have some relatives somewhere in the Loire district. My father met and married my mother when he was stationed in Great Britain during World War Two. So, to that extent, there is a European flavor to the family, but it stops with me. I'm a straight-down-the-line American. My cousins delight in referring to me as 'the Yankee capitalist,' and they're right—I am. I've been all over Europe at one time or another and although I've always enjoyed it, the best part was coming home. I'm afraid what you see here is a true-blue patriot. I love my country."

The devil danced in the eyes that slanted her another quick look, before he added teasingly, "I'm also hung up on American women. I've known, since the time I was old enough to notice girls, that I'd marry an American woman. I've met and, quite frankly, made love to some stunning women all over the world, and yet I wouldn't exchange what I have sitting next to me now for any one of them."

At once pleased and flustered, Tara sought vainly for something to say. When she didn't reply, he went on, "I've inadvertently broken a few Rykovsky family traditions, but there was one I was very happily looking forward to breaking—deliberately."

"What was that?" she murmured, an uneasy premonition snaking up her spine.

"For six generations the Rykovsky brides have been blessed with only one child. A male." Alek paused, and with growing unease Tara watched his jawline tighten, his knuckles whiten as he gripped the steering wheel. "I wanted a son, of course," he went on tersely. "Maybe two. But I also wanted a daughter, possibly more."

Tara found it impossible for a moment to speak

around the lump in her throat. When she did finally get the words out they came jerkily. "I—If you'd agree to a divorce, you could get on with finding a proper mother for your children." She could barely push the last word past the pain in her throat at the sudden vision of a dark-haired little boy with devilish blue eyes. Suddenly her arms ached with painful longing to hold that child close to her breast.

"A proper mother." His low, bitter tone was like a slap across her face, and Tara averted her head to hide the tears that stung her eyes.

He cursed savagely under his breath, then ground out, "I told you the Rykovskys do not divorce. I have no intention of blazing a new trail in that direction." The grim determination in his voice sent a shudder through her. He meant it. He had no intention of giving her her freedom. She felt caught in the trap she'd set herself. They were close to home, and the remaining miles were covered in the hostile silence; the companionable atmosphere of before had been shattered.

Tara lived through the week until Christmas with a growing feeling of unreality. In the short periods of time she and Alek were alone together, they maintained a sort of armed truce. When they were in the company of their respective families or friends, they played the blissfully happy newlyweds.

Tara filled her days by emptying her apartment, disposing of the furniture she didn't want, arranging in Alek's apartment the things she did. And moving her clothes and personal things into the spare bedroom. Alek went back to his office, snapping, "If I remember correctly, your stated wish was that you want nothing from me. I assume that includes my help, so go to it."

Alek rarely came home for dinner and in fact was seldom home by the time she went to bed. It didn't take much speculation on her part to come up with an answer to where he was spending his nights. She spent her own nights alternately hating him, and curled up in bed, arms clutching her midsection, trying to fight down the aching need to feel his arms closing around her, his mouth seeking hers. *God!* she thought. She loved him. And if she had thought she had cried a lot before, she knew now, those tears had been just for openers.

Saturday morning Tara was making her bed when she heard the door to the apartment open, a strange rustling sound, then the door close again. Intrigued, she left the bedroom, walked along the short hall to the living room and stopped, staring in wonder at the live tree Alek had dragged into the room.

Standing the tree straight, he asked blandly, "Do you like it?"

"Yes, of course. I love live Christmas trees, but why?"

"Because it's Christmas," he snapped. "And because, although we won't be doing much entertaining, I'm sure the families will stop over sometime during the holidays. And I don't feel up to lengthy explanations as to why there is none. So," he gestured disinterestedly, "the tree." He then proceeded to surprise her even more by removing a large carton of tree decorations from the storage closet.

Tara tried to show little enthusiasm as she helped him trim the tree. It wasn't easy. She really did love live Christmas trees and had always enjoyed fussing

with the decorations, thinking it one of the best ritu-
als of the holiday. She was also glad she now had a
place to set her gifts. Even if she was a little apprehensive about Alek's reaction to his. As soon as the
tree was finished, Alek showered, dressed, and left the
apartment, telling her he didn't know what time he'd
be back.

On the morning of Christmas Eve Tara stood in
the kitchen dully watching the coffee perk. It was
late, almost eleven, and although she had just awak-
ened, she did not feel rested. She had lain awake,
tense and stiff, until after three in the morning.

The apartment was so still and quiet that Tara was
sure she was alone and so turned with a start when
Alek walked into the kitchen. He looked terrible,
pale and weary with lines of strain around his eyes
and mouth. Tara was torn between deep compassion
and vindictive satisfaction at his obvious exhaustion.

Without a word he walked across the room to her,
then tossed a small, gaily wrapped gift onto the
counter in front of her.

"Your Christmas present," he said shortly. "I'm giving it to you now because I'd like you to wear it to
my parents' party tonight."

Tara eyed the small package with trepidation, then
removed the wrapping with shaking fingers. With
growing alarm she lifted the lid of the tiny, black-vel-
vet-covered box then gasped aloud at the ring nestled
in its bed of white satin. The single sapphire was
large and square-cut and reflected exactly the color of
Alek's eyes.

"Alek, I told you—" she began in a tremulous voice
when he interrupted with a low snarl, "I know what
you told me. But you will wear this, at least in the

169

presence of my parents. They expect it. The Rykovsky men have always adorned their brides with jewels. So you'll do me the favor of wearing it. Not for me, for them. Other than that, I don't care what you do with it. Toss it to the back of a drawer, where it won't offend your eyes."

Tara winced at his harshly bitter tone and, fighting back tears, whispered, "All right, I'll wear it tonight. It—it is beautiful and—"

"Don't strain yourself, Tara, and don't look so frightened, I'm not going to demand payment in return."

Tara had no doubt as to what *payment* he meant, and she turned sharply back to the counter to hide her pain-filled eyes. "Alek, that's not fair." Try as she would, she could not keep the hurt from her voice.

"Not fair?" he snapped. "Lord, I don't believe you said that." Then his tone changed to one of utter weariness. "Oh, the hell with it. I don't want to argue, I have a headache that won't quit and I'm dying of thirst. Isn't that coffee finished yet?"

By the time they left for his parents' party, his bad humor seemed to have vanished along with his headache, and he was his usual controlled, urbane self. Tara wore his ring and tried not to see the cynicism in his eyes as she replied properly to the exclamations of admiration from the other guests.

Christmas morning, still wearing his ring, Tara slipped out of the kitchen as Alek read the paper while drinking his coffee. Gnawing nervously on her lip, she placed his gifts in a neat pile, returned to the kitchen, and set them on the table in front of him. The paper was lowered slowly. Face hard, free of expression, he stared for long moments at the presents before lifting questioning eyes to hers.

"You tell me you'll accept no gifts from me. Then you turn around and buy some *for* me. Why?" Alek's tone confused her, made her feel as if he were asking far more than the actual words stated. For a moment she was tempted to blurt out the truth. That because she loved so deeply she had not been able to resist the urge; she had in fact wanted to buy him the earth.

His eyes, so guarded, so unreadable, stopped her. Swallowing around the dryness in her throat, she managed a careless shrug and answered, "As you said yesterday, it is expected."

The packages were opened silently, his eyes piercing hers each time another lid was lifted. When finally the last one was opened, he stood and came to her, kissed her mouth gently and murmured, "Thank you, Tara. I'm sure our families will be as pleased with your taste and choices as I am."

For a moment he seemed far away, as if caught up in a memory, then he added quietly, "I don't understand you at all, Tara. There are times when I'm sure I have you all figured out, then you say or do something that completely baffles me, and I wonder if I'll ever understand you."

Slowly, over the next few days, as they attended numerous holiday parties and gatherings, she noticed a subtle change in him. It started on Christmas Day, when they made a quick stop at David and Sallie's to deliver their gifts. After unwrapping the exquisite doll they had bought her, the three-year-old Tina had run to Alek, her chubby arms outstretched and laughing, and he had scooped her up into his arms. Tina's small head hid Alek's face from all but Tara, and she felt a hard contraction around her heart at the expression that passed across his face fleetingly as he hugged the child to him. Deep, painful longing had been revealed in that instant, and Tara felt overwhelmed with guilt at her unwillingness to give him the child she now knew he wanted desperately.

From that moment on he seemed to withdraw from her. No longer did she receive his tender glances or softly spoken endearments when in the company of others, and he left her side often and for longer periods of time. By New Year's Eve it became apparent that their friends were aware of his attitude also.

They were attending a rather large party at a private club some distance outside of town and, from the covert glances she was getting, Tara knew her friends were asking themselves if the honeymoon was over. Alek disappeared several times for very long periods, and the fact that Kitty was also conspicuously absent at the same time filled Tara with both jealous fear and embarrassed fury.

Fury conquered fear when midnight came, and then passed, and Tara stood alone in a room full of celebrants kissing and toasting in the new year. Head held high, her step determined, Tara made her way out of the room, ignoring the speculative looks turned her way. She was almost to the cloakroom when she heard a familiar voice call to her to wait and with a sigh she turned and watched Craig Hartman walk up to her. Both his expression and voice held concern.

"Are you leaving?"

She nodded, and when he asked how she was going to get home, she answered briefly, "Taxi."

"No you're not," he stated firmly. "I'll take you."

172

"But—"

He didn't wait to hear her protest but walked into the cloakroom, emerging seconds later shrugging into his coat and carrying hers.

He helped her into her coat then said softly, "Come along," and Tara moved with him out the door, unaware of the alarmed expression that had replaced the usually placid one in David's eyes as he watched them leave.

They drove in silence for about five minutes, then Craig stopped the car on the gravel-covered shoulder of the dark country road. Tara turned in her seat in surprise. "Craig, what—"

"It's not working, is it, Tara?" he interrupted gently.

"Craig, really, I don't want to talk—"

"No, I can understand that," he interrupted again. Then his tone changed, became angry. "But how he could prefer that overblown, destructive bitch over you, I'll never—"

This time it was Tara who interrupted. "Craig, you don't know—"

"No, you're right," he cut in. "But I know her, and she's not worth one minute of your unhappiness."

Before she could think of a reply, Craig added earnestly, "Tara, I told you once that if you ever needed a shoulder to cry on, mine was available. It may not be as broad as his but—"

That was as far as he got, for the door next to Tara was yanked open, her arm was grasped in a grip of steel and she was jerked unceremoniously from her seat. Her outcry was drowned by the low, menacing growl of Alek's voice. "Get the hell out of there and go wait for me in my car."

"Now look here, Rykovsky—" Craig began, only to be cut off by Alek's snarled, "No, *you* look, Hartman." That was all Tara heard before she fled to the T-bird and slid onto the front seat.

CHAPTER TEN

The drive home was completed in ominous quiet, and as soon as she stepped into the apartment, Tara dashed for her bedroom, locking the door behind her. She dropped her coat onto her small rocker then spun around, breath catching in her throat, when she heard Alek call her name and saw the doorknob twist sharply. The next instant her eyes flew wide with disbelief as she heard Alek's foot smash against the door, saw the wood splinter around the lock, and on the second blow from his foot the door slammed back against the wall. Alek's advance on her was reminiscent of the stalk of a predator, and he had the same wild, savage look.

Badly frightened, Tara raised her hands in a defensive movement. With one careless swing of his arm Alek knocked them down then, grasping her upper arms, dragged her roughly against him.

"What is this man to you?" he spat.

"A—a friend," she stuttered.

"He looked *very* friendly," he snarled. His hands moved up and over her shoulders then curled around her throat. "Has he made love to you? The truth, Tara." His fingers tightened and his eyes blazed furiously into hers.

"No! Alek, please," Tara choked.

As if he hadn't heard her, past all reason in his anger, his fingers tightened still more, and Tara groaned softly in pain and fear.

"I'll be damned," he rasped, "if I'll let another man have what's legally mine yet denied me. I could strangle you, Tara, for the hell you've put me through these last weeks."

"Alek, don't," Tara could barely whisper. "I give you my word, I—"

"Damn your doe-soft eyes," he groaned, then his mouth was crushing hers punishingly, bruisingly, as his hand released her throat, slid urgently down her back, molding her body against his.

"Did you really think a locked door would keep me out?" he sneered, when finally his mouth left hers. "Have you been locking your door all this time?"

Shattered, unable to speak, Tara shook her head dumbly.

"Then why tonight?" he asked silkily. "Is there some reason you tried to hide away tonight?"

Tara strove for control, for a measure of calmness in her voice.

"You were so angry. You frightened me, Alek."

"You have every reason to be frightened, my sweet." His soft laugh was not a pretty sound, and his use of the present tense had not escaped her.

"Alek," she breathed desperately, "you can't really believe that I—"

"Can't I?" he cut her off harshly. "Why not? You forget, I held you in my arms all night, felt your response, your need. Whether you admit it to yourself or not, you wanted me as badly as I wanted you. Those needs cannot be turned off like a faucet. I know because right now my body is screaming for possession of yours, and I no longer intend to deny myself that satisfaction."

Tara struggled against him frantically, but it was a losing battle, for in truth she was fighting two opponents, Alek and her own rising desire for him.

Later, lying beside him, replete and spent, she closed her eyes in pain at her own deflections. His possession of her had been as wild and savage as his appearance had been and she had gloried in it, soaking in his lovemaking as thirstily as a drunk slaking his thirst after a long abstinence.

Seconds later a small shiver rippled through her as Alek's lips moved slowly across her cheek then stopped at her own, teasing, tormenting around the outer edge of her mouth, until with a soft moan, she reached up and grasped his head and brought his mouth to her own. When finally he lifted his head, he whispered harshly, "Damn you, Tara, there's no end to my wanting you."

The words, his tone, cut into her like a knife and in self-defense she said fiercely, "I hate you, Aleksei Rykovsky."

He went still for a breathless moment, then his fingers dug painfully into her hair and, his lips close to hers, he groaned, "Well, I guess that's better than indifference. Hate me some more, Tara Rykovsky."

It was late in the morning when Tara woke, wondering why she ached all over. Memory returned in a rush and, turning her head, she gave a long sigh of relief on seeing she was alone. She felt unrested, not very well, and worst of all, used—badly, unjustly used. The thought made her wince, and with a dry sob she covered her face with her hands. Silent tears of conviction running down her face, Tara knew she had to pack and leave, today, before she found herself blabbering her love to Alek like some demented, love-starved idiot, and cringing under his amused triumph.

Giving herself a mental shake, Tara left the bed tiredly, her eyes avoiding the rumpled sheets and covers. Feeling drained, she went to the kitchen and made a pot of coffee, watching it perk dully while she sipped her orange juice. Where was Alek? The answer that presented itself brought pain, and she rejected it with a sharp shake of her head. She didn't know why, but somehow she knew positively that Alek would not leave her bed and go to another woman.

Impatient with the coffeepot, she left the kitchen, stopped at the closet in the short hall, removed her suitcase, and went back to her bedroom. With swift, jerky movements she straightened the bed covers then opened the case on the bed.

For some reason the mild exertion had brought a light film of perspiration to her face and hands and she turned from the case to go to the bathroom. As she stood under the hot, stinging spray in the shower a shudder tore through Tara's body. What was she going to do? For the first time in many years she was uncertain about the direction of her life. Her mind gnawed away at that thought as she dried herself, dressed quickly in jeans and a white rib-knit pullover, and slid her feet into wine-red clogs.

Since her early teens she had set goals for herself and one by one had achieved them. And now all of them seemed unimportant. The thought shook her, and she stopped in the act of placing underwear in her case, her arm motionless in midair. Suddenly she felt very, very old, while at the same time very, very young and she was consumed with the need to talk to someone. Someone older, with more experience of life.

The filmy underthings dropped into the case from numb fingers at the face that flashed into Tara's mind. Her mother? She hadn't sought her mother's counsel since her thirteenth year and yet she had an overriding urge to go to her now.

Before she could change her mind, she hurried into the kitchen to the wall phone there and dialed her mother's number. While the connection was being made and then her mother's phone rang, she poured herself a cup of coffee, only to set it onto the counter with shaking hands when her mother's voice said hello.

"Mama. It's Tara," she said breathlessly, then went on in a rush: "Are you busy? I—I need someone to talk to and I wondered . . . oh, Mama, can I come talk to you? Please?"

There was a short pause, then her mother's voice, strangely calm, came over the wire quietly. "Yes, of course, Tara. Come right away. I'll be waiting for you."

Hands still shaking badly, Tara replaced the receiver; she dashed into the bedroom, shrugged into a Navy pea jacket, scooped up her handbag, and left the apartment. The untouched coffee sat cooling on the counter; the half filled suitcase lay open on her bed; the dresser drawers remained ajar.

On entering her father's house, Tara stood inside the door, glancing around in question at the unusual quiet.

"I'm in the kitchen, Tara," her mother called. "Come have a cup of coffee."

Marlene Schmitt stood at the sink, pouring coffee into two heavy earthenware mugs and, as Tara seated herself at the table, she turned and said, "We can talk here. Betsy is spending the day with Kenny and his parents, and your father took the boys out to give us some privacy."

"Mother!" Tara exclaimed. "You didn't say anything to Dad, did you?"

Marlene's eyebrows went up as she sat down opposite Tara. Then, her tone slightly chiding, she murmured, "There wasn't much I could tell him, other than that you seemed upset and were coming over to talk. He didn't ask questions, simply gathered up the boys and left."

Tara eyed her mother wonderingly as she sipped her coffee. Never before could she remember hearing quite that calm, unruffled tone and for the moment she was left speechless. Her next words left her stunned.

"Your father is not the unfeeling brute you think he is, Tara." And when Tara tried to speak out in protest, her mother held up her hand and added, "Nor am I quite the blind fool. No, don't interrupt. Please, let me finish. Failure to do all you'd like to for your family can do strange things to some men, and that is what has happened to your father. I've watched it happening for a long time. But he is a good man, Tara. I love him. I always have."

Tara stared at her mother as if at a stranger. Had she been wrong all these years? Misread the situation? She had thought her mother stayed with her father

180

because of her and her sister and brothers, and out of a sense of duty. But now?

Marlene's soft voice brought her attention back to the present and her own situation.

"There's a problem with Alek, isn't there?"

Looking at her mother through different eyes, Tara felt her throat close and she whispered, "Yes."

"I thought so. I have for some time now. For all your bright smiles and happy chatter, I knew you were unhappy. And so is Alek."

"Mama, you don't understand," Tara cried. And her mother came back, "Possibly not, but I understand this. Alek is a bright, ambitious, very attractive man. And he is a man, Tara. The kind of man who needs a mature woman beside him. One who is willing to give, as well as take."

Tara felt tears sting her eyelids. Was that the type of woman that, in her single-mindedness, she had projected? One who was not willing to give? Before she could form an argument, her mother said, "Less than a month ago you made a commitment to that man. Have you lived up to it?"

Vision blurred by tears, unable to speak, Tara shook her head.

"Honey, do you love him?"

Tears now unashamedly running down her cheeks, Tara sobbed, "Yes. Oh, Mama, yes. But he doesn't love me." She paused, then added bitterly, "He says he wants me, and that's not the same, is it?"

"No, it isn't," Marlene answered very softly, her fingers brushing gently at the tears. "But that's something, and as long as there's something, some emotion, there's reason to work at it. It probably won't be easy, Tara. But then nothing worth having ever does come easy."

As Tara drove back to the apartment, her mind went over what her mother said. There had been more, much more, but in essence, what it had amounted to was this: Tara had worked hard for everything she had wanted; surely the one thing she wanted most in the world was worth twice the work.

Tara was still unsure of what she'd do or say to Alek, if anything, when she got home. But she was grateful for one thing: This new and deeper understanding between her mother and herself. She had been on her own for some time; now, for the first time, she felt really grown-up.

Suddenly Tara knew she was not yet ready to go home. She had to think this through, make a decision one way or the other. Eyes steady on the road, she drove into the mountains. All the splendor of fall was gone now, but even denuded of their summer finery, the Poconos were a balm to her mind.

Time slipped by unnoticed as did the large and small billboards advertising the lodges, motels, and many points of interest and activities offered.

Her mind drove on in rhythm with the car's engine, paging back over the last few months, going over everything, step by step. And over and over, threading through her thoughts, her mother's voice asked softly, *"Honey, do you love him?"*

What should she do? The events leading up to this day, many of which were caused by Alek, no longer held any importance. The question driving her on now was: *Did* he still want her? Her throat still hurt from the pressure of his fingers last night. Every muscle in her body felt sore. She felt sure he had not

182

set out to make love to her, but to punish her. He had been rough with her, as if deliberately acting out the role of savage she'd cast him in. His stated intention had been to own her. Now that he did, had he lost interest?

He had become so cool, so withdrawn over the last week. A shudder rippled through her as she remembered the previous Thursday. She had left the office to find a mist-shrouded fairyland of ice, glittering and treacherous. She had driven home at a mere crawl, holding her breath each time she felt the tires lose their grip and begin to slide. By the time she had shut off the engine inside the apartment building's covered parking area, her palms and forehead were damp with sweat, and she had felt totally exhausted.

As she'd thrust her key into the apartment door, she'd had one thought in mind: to soak in a hot tub and forget that world of ice outside. She took one step through the doorway when Alek's voice rapped, "Where the hell have you been?"

He was standing at the bar, phone at his ear, his one palm covering the mouthpiece. Before she could answer, his hand slid away and he said shortly, "Yes, it's her."

Just as she was about to close the door, Tara had stopped, frozen by his next words.

"Yes, Kitty, I know, but I don't know what else to tell you. Perhaps in a week, maybe less."

What had possessed her? Even now Tara didn't know. At the time she had not stopped to think, to ask for an explanation. She had run out of the apartment to her car and back to that ice-covered world that had nothing on her heart.

How long she'd slithered around aimlessly, she had no idea, but when finally she had turned back to the apartment, it was raining hard, the ice fast disappearing. There was no sign of Alek when she got back, and as she soaked in the tub, Tara wondered dully if he was with Kitty. The searing pain of jealousy she'd felt on the night she'd first realized she was in love with him was nothing compared to the agony she'd gone through while sliding around on the glassy streets. And now, tired to the bone, she was almost beyond feeling.

She was lying on the bed, staring at the ceiling, her bedside lamp still on, when she heard the front door slam moments before Alek was standing in her doorway, face cold, eyes blazing.

"How long have you been here?"

"A—a half hour or so."

"While I've been running around nearly killing myself looking for you." His voice had been ugly, not much more than a snarl. "Would that have made your revenge complete, I wonder?"

"Alek, please, I'm sorry—"

But it had been too late; he was gone, slamming out of the apartment as violently as he'd entered.

Tara's hands gripped the wheel as she shivered again. Vaguely she registered the road sign indicating the number of miles to Camelback. Then last night, she wondered, had his neglect, indifference, been his way of showing her he no longer cared if she left him? got a divorce? But then why had he been so angry about Craig? His pride? Of course. She could hear him now. *"Has he made love to you?"* That fierce Rykovsky pride would not be able to bear the

184

thought of someone else having what he still called his own. The thoughts swirled and whirled, leading nowhere.

Camelback!! Good grief, she had to turn this car around, go home. And there was her answer, clear as a perfect spring day. She had to go home, and Alek was all the home she ever wanted. Silently she answered her mother's question. *Yes, Mama, I love him. More than I ever thought it possible to love any one person. I'm afraid, Mama, so afraid. For if he no longer wants me, I no longer want to live.*

Alek's car was parked in the apartment lot and with trembling fingers, Tara let herself into the apartment. She stood listening to the silence in the empty living room a moment then, slipping off her jacket, she went to her bedroom to stand staring at the open case on her bed. Alek's voice, from the doorway, went through her like an electric shock.

"Where have you been?"

"Alek, I—"

"No. Never mind. As long as you're all right. The way you left the apartment, I thought something had happened." His voice was so cool, so withdrawn, Tara shivered. His eyes left her face, rested long moments on the suitcase, then came back to hers. "Before you leave, I have something to say to you. If you'll come into the living room, please?"

He turned and walked away, and Tara was left staring at the empty doorway, fingers of real fear digging at her stomach. She didn't know what he had to say, but she was almost positive she didn't want to hear it and she actually had to force herself to follow him.

He was standing gazing out of the window when

she entered the room, and the sight of him clutched at her heart. Why, of all the men she had known, did it have to be this one who could rob the strength from her knees, make her ache in anticipation? He was everything she had avowed she had not wanted in a man, yet he was the only man she wanted.

He was standing very straight, almost stiff, and as he turned from the window, Tara felt the breath catch in her throat. His face had an austere, lifeless cast and the usually glittering blue eyes looked flat, empty. His eyes went over her slowly as if studying every detail, and when he finally spoke, it was in that same cool, withdrawn tone.

"I'm a proud man, Tara, as you know. This is possibly the hardest thing I'll ever have to say, and I'll only say it one time. Don't leave me." He paused and his tone became softer. "I beg you, stay with me. I give you my word I'll do everything in my power to make it a good life for both of us."

Eyes wide with astonishment, Tara stared at him, unable to move for a full fifteen seconds. Then, with a small incoherent cry, she was across the room, flinging herself against his chest.

"Oh, Alek," she whispered. "And here I was, about to beg you to let me stay."

"Let you stay?" he repeated incredulously, his arms hard and tight around her. "I never wanted you to go. You know that. I've been berating myself all day for what happened last night. For giving you what I thought was the perfect excuse for leaving me."

Her hand slid underneath his pullover, then up and over his warm skin, with an urgency in her to touch him. She felt a shudder ripple through his body as he buried his face in her hair and groaned,

186

"Oh, God, Tara, I love you. I swear if I ever walk in again and find your suitcase open, I *will* strangle you. These few weeks have been pure hell, wanting to hold you like this all the time I tried to work during the day, lying alone in that damn bed at night."

"Which reminds me," Tara stepped back and looked up into eyes now alive and glowing with love and tenderness. "Where have you been every night? You didn't spend very many hours alone in that bed."

"Are you jealous, Tara?" he laughed down at her.

"Yes, damn you. And what were you and Kitty up to last night?"

He laughed again, kissed her fast and hard, then said softly, "Simmer down, hellion, and don't swear at me. Kitty wants to open her own boutique and needed some backing. I've looked over her plans and decided to invest. And that's all."

"On New Year's Eve?" she cried in disbelief.

"Well, I may have been trying to punish you a little. Damn it, Tara, you've been driving me crazy for months. I thought, after that unbelievable wedding night, that you'd realize what you meant to me. What you have meant to me since not long after I met you. In the last week I've felt at the end of my wits and patience. It was either stay away from you or drag you off to the nearest bed. It seems I did both."

He stopped long enough to give her another hard kiss, then a little shake. "As for Kitty. There is nothing between us but business. Anything else was over some time ago. And she never lived in this apartment or slept in our bed." His arms loosened and his hands came up to cup her face, long fingers sliding into her hair. Lips close to hers, he rasped, "Tara, if you don't soon tell me you love me, I won't be responsible for my actions."

Soft brown eyes gazed into anxious blue ones then, quietly, but very clearly, Tara said. "I love you, Alek."

"Dear God," he moaned. "I was beginning to think I'd never hear you say it." Then his mouth was crushing hers, his hands moving down her back, molding the softness of her body to the hard strength of his. Tara's mind whirled, then the room spun as he scooped her into his arms and strode into the bedroom. Their bedroom.

As he lowered her gently onto the bed, Tara whispered, "Since right after you met me, Alek?"

"Yes, pansy eyes."

"But, I don't understand."

"Oh, Tara. You were so cold. You seemed to take such an aversion to me. I guess, at first, my vanity was stung. I made up my mind to find out more about you."

Kicking off his shoes, he slid onto the bed beside her, then proceeded to drive her slightly mad with tiny, fervent kisses, until she caught at his head and pulled it back with a pleaded, "Alek?"

"All right," he sighed. One long finger tracing the contours of her face, he went on. "It didn't take long to find out you went out only with men who had— ah—shall we say, good prospects? But somehow that didn't seem to quite fit you. So I dug a little deeper, observed a little harder, and came up with the answer. You were scared to death of strong-willed men. By then I was so damn in love, I knew I had to have you, by whatever methods. But how to get close to you, get under the fence you'd built around yourself?

You avoided me whenever possible, cut me dead whenever I spoke to you. That's when I put my plan into motion. I didn't want to hurt you, for when you hurt, I hurt. But I did want you."

"And in all this time, until today, that's all you've said. 'I want you.'"

"Not true, pansy eyes. I've been telling you I loved you since the first night I came to your apartment. I knew you were not yet ready to hear it, so I said it in Russian. If you remember the morning after our wedding I said I had something to tell you when I asked you to come back to bed. I was fully prepared to lay my heart and my life at your feet. In English."

"Those Russian words!" Tara exclaimed. "But how could I know?"

Then, her arms snaking around his neck, she whispered, "Translate at once—please."

Alek's breath was a cool caress against her mouth as he murmured the Russian words, then whispered, "Roughly translated, it's 'My darling, Tara, I love you.'"

Dell Bestsellers